Kiss and tell

A SWEETEST KISSES NOVELLA

GRACE BURROWES

NEW YORK TIMES BESTSELLING AUTHOR

Kiss and Tell by Grace Burrowes

Cover Design by Wax Creative, Inc

ISBN: 978-1-941419-10-6

Published by:
 Grace Burrowes Publishing
21 Summit Avenue
Hagerstown, MD 21740
Graceburrowes.com

Printed and published in the United States.

CHAPTER ONE

"Scheduled sex! This divorce is about scheduled sex, Mr. Cromarty. I did not bear that man two children, give up a promising teaching career, and move five hundred miles from my family so I could *subsist* on scheduled sex. Scheduled *missionary* sex."

Scheduled sex sounded lovely to Dunstan Cromarty, attorney-at-law. A bit of anticipation, maybe flirtation over a good meal, some guaranteed peace and quiet, privacy. No bringing a lady home on a rare, lucky evening to find Wallace had just used the litter box and perfumed the entire downstairs.

"I told Calvin I'd put that in the legal complaint," Mrs. Almquist went on. "About the scheduled sex. Twice a week, unless Cal was at some accountant's conference. Then I got a rain check. I told Calvin what he could do with his rain checks."

A moment of sympathy for poor Calvin threatened, though Dunstan allowed none of it to show on his face. Seventeen years of missionary sex might try any lady's patience, after all.

Unless the alternative was no sex at all.

"If we settle your case," Dunstan said, "we won't need to bring up those particulars in the filings, and the great majority of family law cases do settle. How old are the children?"

On his trusty yellow legal pad, sitting at a conference

table easily four times his age, Dunstan took down the usual information—family of four, one income, though it was a certified public accountant's executive income, low-interest mortgage, tidy retirement assets incubating in a variety of accounts, and—in these trying times, with the marriage crumbling—the Almquists had *no debt.*

"Do you suspect your husband has any hidden assets, Mrs. Almquist?"

"Call me Dorie. Yes, he has hidden assets. Calvin's sense of humor hasn't been spotted in since the youngest was eight, and I'm pretty sure Cal still has a nice ass."

A low, grinding ache started up at the base of Dunstan's spine, for this was going to be one of *those* divorces. "What about financial assets he's trying to keep from your notice?"

"No. Calvin is literally an Eagle Scout. Cheerful, loyal, thrifty, brave. *Missionary.*"

God help the Eagle Scout when his missus craved a three-doggie night.

"Transparency of finances can make a divorce proceeding much simpler," Dunstan said. "Discovery will proceed more smoothly, and the division of assets won't become a quagmire of motions and hearings."

"What's discovery?"

He explained about the documents that had to be exchanged—financial records, check registers, bank statements, tax filings, anything that might shed light on the couple's financial situation, or their fitness to parent.

With the Almquists, that picture ought to emerge fairly easily.

He was delivering good news, in so far as any aspect of any divorce could be good news, but Mrs. Almquist was swinging her foot like she desperately needed the loo.

She was a ferociously well maintained female—tasteful highlights in honey-blond hair, a toned figure showing to good advantage in a teal and brown pantsuit, and nails lacquered to match her silk shell. Makeup subtly minimized the approach of her thirty-seventh birthday, and her shoes would probably have paid for two new tires on Dunstan's truck.

"Do you date, Mr. Cromarty?"

She was also furious and broken-hearted.

"I'm too busy to date and I never date clients or former clients." Or lawyers, or the good ladies who worked at the courthouse, which left…Wallace and the remote, most Saturday nights.

Sometimes he'd liven things up with poker night at Trent Knightley's, but the camaraderie among the three Knightley brothers had a way of hollowing the bonhomie the gathering was intended to create. For Dunstan had brothers of his own, far, far, away.

"I wasn't hitting on you," *Dorie* said, though her expression suggested she'd consider him for escort service. "You're good-looking, in a tall, dark, handsome, green-eyed way. I was wondering what it's like *out there*, now. I haven't dated anybody but Calvin for the past seventeen years, and things change."

She'd changed, was what she meant, and some of those changes frightened her.

"You're still married," Dunstan said, kindly, because she didn't *feel* married. She likely felt trapped, betrayed, and exhausted. "Unless you want to give Mr. Almquist the fault ground of adultery upon which to proceed, I suggest you let the dating wait."

In Damson Valley, a close-knit rural community within commuting distance of both Washington and Baltimore, dating was best done openly or not at all.

"I will be damned if I'll give that man anything other than what the law says he's entitled to, and not one penny more."

Oh, this case would be great fun. Drug dealers were a pleasure to represent compared to embittered spouses who had the means to torment each other in family court. Criminals understood the rules, paid cash, and referred all three dozen of their closest friends.

Wallace would be ashamed of his owner for such thoughts.

"Have you considered counseling, Mrs. Almquist?"

"Marriage counseling? Like when you have to tell some stranger all the intimate details of your failed relationship? No, thank you. I might hate Calvin, but I wouldn't put him through that. Marriages are private."

Of course, they were. While divorces…

Dunstan turned over a clean sheet on his tablet. "I was thinking more in terms of giving you emotional support to help you sort through your situation. Divorce can be daunting, and some therapists specialize in assisting couples through the divorce itself."

Devastating was the honest term.

Her foot went abruptly still. "I'm not a whiner, Mr. Cromarty. Ask my spin class. Full speed ahead and get the hills behind me, that's me."

"Then my first job will be to contact Calvin's attorney and ask if he or she will accept service of process on your behalf."

The foot started up again. "He's hiring some woman. Women attorneys make less than men, on average, according to Calvin, and he gets off on pinching pennies. I wish just once he'd pinch my behind."

How plaintive she sounded. Heaven defend the good bachelors of Damson Valley when Dorie Almquist's divorce became final. Might be a good time to nip back to Scotland and spend a few weeks fly-fishing, sipping whiskey, and dandling wee baby cousins.

"Do you happen to know the name of your husband's attorney?"

"She had a dull name, like a third grade teacher."

Which narrowed matters down not at all. "Hannah Stark is a new associate with Hartman and Whitney, though I doubt she'd be taking her own cases yet."

"Not Hannah. Judy something, or Jane. Jane—that's it. As

in plain Jane."

If the woman made another comment about missionary sex, Dunstan would hand her back her retainer check, though it would pain him to turn away business.

"Jane DeLuca?"

"That's it. Plain Jane DeLuca. I'll bet she wears sensible shoes, with a name like that."

"Ms. DeLuca is a fine attorney, very professional. I'll give her a call this afternoon."

Mrs. Almquist left in a flurry of fruity perfume and indignation, while Dunstan took his notes back to his office and popped a couple of aspirin before his back started howling at him.

He'd never before taken a case against Ms. Jane DeLuca, but by reputation she *was* very professional—for a land-dwelling shark—and even in the courtroom, *especially* in the courtroom, she wore stilettos.

***

"What will this divorce cost me?"

The clients always asked, as if the model without the chrome hubcaps might be the better deal.

Jane DeLuca, Es-flipping-squire, always had an answer for them.

"The cost of your divorce depends on four variables, only one of which you control."

Oncologists and attorneys had a lot in common. Both learned to talk about awful truths, right down to the clinical details, without touching on the awful emotions. Too bad nobody ever made that plain to law school applicants until after the loans had come due.

Calvin Almquist adjusted a gold and onyx cuff link that looked like it might commemorate graduation from some Ivy League university.

"Those four variables are?"

Jane launched into the standard spiel, of which Calvin

would retain about a third, if he was like most clients enduring the trauma of inchoate divorce.

"So you're saying I can't control the legal complexity of my case, I can't control my spouse, and I can't control whom she chooses to represent her, but I can control my own behavior."

That would be a stretch, given that divorce made brokenhearted, angry fools of most mortals.

"You choose our litigation objective, Mr. Almquist. If you want sole custody, I'll go after that, hammer and tongs. If you want this divorce wrapped up quickly, then you may see your children only every other weekend, but we won't allow the case to get bogged down in litigation. If a cordial relationship with your ex is the highest priority,"—Calvin winced, tellingly—"then this might take forever, and you could still see your kids only every other weekend, but cordial it will be. You choose the objective."

"I want to have enough to live on, but I need to be a father to my children, too."

Which—surely a coincidence!—was exactly what a solid marriage often fostered.

"Both of those goals are sensible and important. You may need to choose between them."

Rather than prattle on about the court calendar, the procedural details—yes, a divorce was a lawsuit—Jane gave Calvin a moment to absorb a bit more of his *new normal*.

Which had to be one of the most hated euphemisms in the language.

Divorce involved choices, usually between two or more bad alternatives. The first choice, however, after the decision to split, was which lawyers had the privilege of presiding over the internment of the marriage.

"So you can't tell me what the divorce will cost?"

It will cost you your marriage, your remaining complement of innocence, and possibly your life savings—but what will that matter when your children are in rehab?

"I can give you estimates." Jane moved away from her desk to touch the soft, prickly moss in her window dish garden. Calvin looked like what he was: a successful accountant—regular features, tidy dark hair, about five-foot-ten with an "I work out Monday, Wednesday and Friday mornings" trimness. He would read accounting magazines on the stationary bike and have no balances on either of his two credit cards.

Jane used a porcelain Eeyore pitcher to water the dish garden, then topped up a bouquet of yellow and pink tulips Louise had sent at the beginning of the week.

"You'll bill me monthly?"

"If you decide to give me your case, and if I decide to take it, I will bill you against a retainer."

When she got around to doing the billing. Louise, the traitor, had always handled that aspect of the business.

Calvin stood, jingling the change in his left pocket. "But you can't tell me what it will cost, how long it will go on, or what the outcome will be. I hate this, and none of it is my fault."

No divorce was ever anybody's fault, not until some time had passed, a good therapist or two had gone to work, and the judgments were all final.

Jane put Eeyore on the credenza, a reminder that he needed a refill.

"Think of this divorce as a disease, Mr. Almquist. You may have done nothing to deserve it, but if you don't take the situation seriously, you will not like the outcome."

Though Jane had never met the couple comprised of a blameless angel married to an irredeemable devil. Still, she sympathized with Calvin, who probably hadn't done anything *on purpose* to sabotage his marriage. He'd be both bewildered and ashamed to find himself in a lawyer's office for anything other than the drafting of a will.

"Is the retainer negotiable?"

Five years ago, Jane would have taken that bait. She would

have returned to her desk and asked him how much he could manage, while she drove on bald tires and had no health insurance.

"I'm good at what I do, Mr. Almquist. If I represent you, you will get good value for your coin. Neither one of us wants you wondering if my zeal in the courtroom is affected by the outstanding balance you owe me. The retainer is not negotiable, and may I point out, that retainer would buy you a lot of marriage counseling."

He left off jingling the coins. "Dorie won't go for that. She has her pride, and she's an excellent mother. She and I have managed seventeen mostly good years. We'll manage this too."

"Are you sure this isn't just a rough patch, Mr. Almquist? Seventeen years is a notorious spike in the chart for divorces."

"Dorie is sure. Frequently in error but seldom in doubt, like the British monarchy. I used to love that about her."

Dorie had probably loved that Calvin was on top of every penny, all the time, rather than a lackadaisical spendthrift like, for example, her own father.

Calvin pushed thick glasses up a nose that would have been nice, if he weren't making a not-nice-at-all face.

"Dorie won't like you one bit. She's insecure about her looks and her education, and you're pretty *and* well educated."

He made Jane's red hair and blue eyes—tired blue eyes—sound like a walking affront to the decency police.

"If Mrs. Almquist attempts to antagonize me, that can work to your advantage."

He resumed his seat, laid a steel briefcase across his lap, and snapped the locks. "How much did you say the retainer is?"

He had a checkbook out, a sign not of sound decision-making ability, but rather, of a man who found every moment of the discussion acutely painful, if not infuriating.

"We need to go over the retainer agreement first," Jane said, gently, gently, because this guy had *high maintenance* written all over him, *if* she decided to represent him.

Which she would, because Louise had left the practice, while the rent bill still occupied a place on Jane's payables ledger.

Calvin tolerated the next hour well, despite Jane's misgivings, and thus she did, eventually, agree to represent him. His documents would be organized and timely produced, his check would not bounce, and he'd likely keep his pants on for the duration of the festivities.

A family law attorney learned not to expect much from her clients.

"When will we file?" Calvin asked.

We. Already, Jane had been promoted to *we* status, with Calvin her wingman in the halls of justice, though the last time he'd been to the county courthouse had probably been to buy his marriage license.

"I will meet with you on Friday and have a draft petition ready by Tuesday, though I warn you, couples do reconcile, Mr. Almquist. Seventeen years is a lot to walk away from, especially when you have children to consider. If you do get back together, the unused portion of the retainer will be returned to you."

For an instant, sheer misery shone out of Calvin's brown eyes. He wasn't Jane's type—she didn't have a type—but once, long ago, dear Dorie had thought those eyes attractive. Intelligent, at least, which counted for a lot with some women.

"Until Friday, then." He stuck out a hand, and Jane shook, because business civilities in the midst of domestic tragedy comforted some clients.

"Call me if you have any questions," Jane said, seeing him to the door. They all had questions, and who could blame them?

Speaking of which. "Did you say who Dorie's attorney is, Mr. Almquist?"

Calvin took his raincoat off the coat stand and fit a beret

onto his head. "Dorie retained some guy named Dunstan Cromarty. I think he's Scottish."

"Mr. Cromarty is Scottish, also very professional. He'll advocate for Doreen zealously within the bounds of the law."

And from what Jane had heard, Cromarty would be a perfect, if entirely civil, pain in the ass about it, every step of the way.

***

One of the law clerks had asked Jane why she preferred to work in the law library when she'd already memorized the entire Family Law Article of the Annotated Code of Maryland.

"Because you never know when you might need to start on Courts and Judicial Proceedings." She'd memorized only certain articles because she referred to them constantly.

The kid had backed away. *Backed* away.

"I was told I'd find you here." Dunstan Cromarty stood before the table Jane had taken over in the Damson County law library, his battered leather case in hand.

"I like books," Jane said. She was prepared to not like Dunstan Cromarty, though he nicely filled out a medium-blue three-piece suit that had to have been hand-tailored. "Stop looming. If you must interrupt me, then take a seat."

He folded long limbs into a sturdy wooden chair that had likely been in the county courthouse when the Confederate Army had marched by on their way to Gettysburg. "Don't suppose you're working on the Almquist divorce complaint." His burr made even his oh-so-casual question sexy.

She could fence with him, but she'd been talking with other attorneys who practiced family law in Damson County. With Dunstan Cromarty, battles should be chosen, not engaged in for the hell of it.

"And *if* I were working on the Almquist filings?"

He slouched back. "The case will not be pleasant."

Beneath the table, Jane fished for her shoes, but one didn't surreptitiously slip into stilettos. "Domestic cases are seldom pleasant."

His aftershave was *pleasant*. Subtle, fresh, spicy. An outdoorsy scent that went with his burr, which—Jane admitted—she *did* like. Rather a lot. Judges and juries were said to like that burr too.

"The Almquist divorce will be a right stinker," Cromarty said. "I'm hoping you'll accept service of process, though I'm perfectly happy to serve dear Calvin at the gym, in his office, or at his Toastmasters gathering."

Any accent originating in the British Isles gave its speaker an advantage in matters of irony—dear Calvin, indeed. Jane put her computer into sleep mode and folded down the screen.

"Why don't I serve dear Doreen at her gym, or her garden club, or in the privacy of her fifty-five-hundred-square-foot marital home?" If Jane had had her shoes on, she would have stood to pose that query.

"Because Dorie—I'm to call her Dorie—would take it out on her lawyer, as would Calvin, should he suffer the humiliation of public service with a divorce complaint."

Cromarty had directed his irony at himself, or possibly the entire legal profession, while Jane's sweet little smart-pad with a mighty battery gave a soft, cyber-sigh.

"Sometimes, I think having the client accept service in person is better," Jane said, when a simple yes or no might have done. "They need to take the litigation seriously, need to know it will wreck their lives."

"Is that a warning, Ms. DeLuca?"

Drat him. A glimmer of collegial commiseration, followed by a sneering jab. Except Cromarty was smiling. One corner of his mouth had tipped up, and green eyes regarded Jane with as much humor as challenge.

Had she ever seen him smile before? "I'll accept process if you will."

"We are agreed, then. Will you be at the bar lunch on Tuesday?"

Good Lord, was it already time for that monthly ordeal?

"I should be there, though rubber chicken on wilted lettuce isn't exactly my speed." Particularly not if Elvin Gregory plunked himself down beside her again and began with one of his infamous "I once had a case…" monologues.

"We can trade complaints then, maybe do a bit of strategizing."

Her right toe snagged a heel strap, and Jane began wiggling her foot into the shoe. "I'm opposing counsel, Cromarty. What will we strategize about?"

"Scheduling, if nothing else. This case will fall across the winter holidays, and I like to go home to Scotland for Hogmanay."

A little bend, a yank with her index finger, and the right shoe was on. Now for the left.

"What's Hog Many?" And where was home, exactly? Scotland, but where in Scotland? Where, for that matter, was her left shoe?

"*Hogmanay*. New Year's. We set great store by new beginnings in Scotland. So many of us have had to make them. Did you just caress my foot with your toes?"

She had. "Of course not. Your foot got in the way while I'm trying to find my shoe."

He reached a long arm under the table and—"Watch it, Cromarty!"—came up with Jane's left shoe in his hand.

"Interesting." He studied the shoe, an elegant aubergine four-incher Jane had bought for a steal at a consignment shop in Rockville. "These cannot be comfortable. One wonders how you march about the courtrooms in them with such apparent ease. Bad for the knees, these things, and they lead to bunions."

The shoes were dead sexy. Not do-me shoes, but I-might-*let*-you-do-me-*if*-you're-really-good shoes. That Dunstan Cromarty was inspecting Jane's shoe at eye level was not comfortable.

Jane used the law library because people frequented the place. People who might pass the time of day with her, or need a hint where the Atlantic Second Reporters were shelved. People who made quiet, comforting people-nearby noises without troubling her. She'd have to find somewhere else to work that didn't leave her open to attacks from Highland shoe pirates.

"Give me my shoe."

He hesitated a single instant before passing over the shoe, the smile becoming a damned dimple in his left cheek. "We aren't truly about to wreck the Almquist's lives, are we, Ms. DeLuca?"

She jerked the shoe on, though the strap was twisted when she straightened. "No, we are not. They've already seen to that themselves. Now, if you'll excuse me, I have a complaint for limited divorce to draft."

He rose, the only guy in the Damson County bar association who carried off a three-piece suit, matching tie tack and French cuffs as if that was simply what one wore.

"I'll be at work on the complementary accusations from Mrs. Almquist and look forward to seeing you Tuesday."

He sauntered off, the view from the back being elegant, strong, and… Elegant and strong were bad enough. Cromarty played fair, but he played to win. Mrs. Almquist had chosen her advocate well.

Mr. Almquist had chosen better, though, because when it came to divorce litigation, Jane wasn't *playing.* She'd make it a point to sit next to Mr. Cromarty at lunch on Tuesday, the better to impress that upon him.

She collected her effects and rose, then nearly fell on her backside when the strap to her left shoe broke.

***

Scotland was usually five hours ahead of Maryland, which meant Dunstan often talked to his mother directly after lunch. Mum liked to watch her shows on the telly, and yet, if she didn't periodically get in "a good natter" with her prodigal son, she fretted.

"So mind you don't embroil me in one of your appellate arguments," he told Trenton Knightley, another family law practitioner whom he occasionally opposed. "I've work to do this afternoon, unlike you lot."

Knightley got the door to the Steak and Anvil, where the bar association gathered for its monthly lunches. "Do you think my brothers would allow me to malinger here over expensive beer and tough steak when I could be back at the office, clocking billable hours?"

Rubber chicken and wilted lettuce for some.

"The shoe is likely on the other foot, Knightley. You herd your brothers back to the office, though why we must have a speaker each month is beyond fathoming."

Knightley wiggled dark brows. "We're supposed to finish planning the details of the bar association's Christmas party today too. Have you been a good boy, Cromarty?"

Americans and their endless self-disclosure. "Very good, though it's none of your ruddy business. Shall you do the motion on the Baxter guardianship or shall I?"

The hostess waved to the banquet room, which was about the size of Dunstan's garage.

"You consent to naming the daughter guardian of Baxter's person?"

"I defer to the court. Any one of the children would serve competently. Send me the draft order before you file the motion, though."

"You have issues with trust, Cromarty," Knightley said as they reached the banquet room. "I'll have the order to you by the end of the week."

Every competent attorney had issues with trust, as well as a fine command of language, at least when on the clock. Trent Knightley was a good fellow, and yet, two heads were better than one when it came to drafting court orders.

"Your brothers are waving you over, Knightley." James and MacKenzie Knightley, the corporate and criminal specialists in the Knightley brothers' law firm, were drinking imported beer at the end of the middle table. Both were agreeable men and superbly competent in their fields.

"Sit with us. We'll break into a chorus of *Jingle Bells* when Elvin Gregory starts holding forth on."

They would, too, and probably make it harmonize.

"I'm promised to Ms. DeLuca, though thank you."

"Poker on Saturday," Knightley said, saluting his brothers. "Mac's springing for the pizza, and it's your turn to lose."

Dunstan did not wave to Ms. DeLuca, who'd taken an end seat at the far table. She had her little computer out of its pink case, not a laptop, but one of the smaller varieties made for people with small hands, perfect eyesight and untreated compulsive tendencies.

"Ms. DeLuca, I have it on good authority this gathering will degenerate into a planning session for the annual bar Christmas party, which I will not be attending. Might I convince you to join me in an elopement?"

She slapped her computer closed and jammed it in an oversize shoulder bag, from which a pair of manila legal briefs peeked, one of which was labeled "Almquist, Calvin."

"You didn't mean that the way it sounded," she said, rising. "You can't help that you still don't speak American, but yes, I'll *elope* with you. Just don't tell our clients."

She preceded him through the private dining room, and yes, Dunstan watched the part of her a gentleman shouldn't watch in public. A glance around the room confirmed that the Damson County Bar Association was sadly lacking in gentlemen, and the ladies present were not surprised to find it so.

Both Dunstan's mum and Wallace would have been ashamed of him, but his brothers and cousins would have understood.

He held the door for Ms. DeLuca, a short exercise in confusion on her part and patience on his, and then they were outside on a pleasant autumn day. Yellow leaves scraped along the sidewalk, and sunlight slanted sharply through bare branches overhead.

"Where are we eloping to?" she asked. "I have the Complaint for Limited Divorce, but I'm also hungry."

She wasn't simply American, she was Jane DeLuca: Here's your lawsuit, I'll take fries with that.

"I have Mrs. Almquist's too, though I'm not sure filing this soon is the appropriate approach. Will you share an Eritrean meal with me?"

Because Eritrean fare—a rare treat in rural Maryland—done right was a wonderful break from sandwiches consumed standing up in the kitchen after the cat had been fed. Even Ms. DeLuca's dubious company couldn't douse Dunstan's longing for a culinary change of pace.

"Haven't had Ethiopian since I moved out here from DC," Ms. DeLuca said, marching off across the street. "A good dose of carbs sounds perfect, and why shouldn't we be filing complaints, getting the ball rolling, starting discovery?"

He hauled her back by the strap of her purse as an orange scooter came barreling around the corner, and in her fancy shoes, she teetered for a moment, then righted herself.

"A simple, 'watch your step' would do, Mr. Cromarty."

"I beg your pardon." The dratted woman would injure herself in those ridiculous shoes, and why did she bother with them, when even in her heels, she came only to Dunstan's shoulder?

This time, she looked both ways before proceeding, and let him hold the door for her when they reached the restaurant.

"A table or a booth?" the hostess asked.

"Table," from Ms. DeLuca, of course.

"I'd prefer a booth, for privacy, and in case we have to spread out any paperwork." Also to be contrary, because exploring the other side's weaknesses was good strategy and half the fun of being an attorney.

"A booth will do," Ms. DeLuca said. "Though you'd better not spill anything on my files, Cromarty."

Or she'd what? Hit him with her Lawyer Barbie computer?

"I'll be quite tidy," Dunstan said, because he was always tidy. The other benefit of a booth—or detriment, depending on a fellow's perspective—was that it mooted the whole dilemma of whether to hold the lady's chair.

"Would Madam like silverware?" the waitress inquired, when they'd settled in a corner booth. She had a musical, slightly French accent, four gold hoops in her right ear, and a friendly smile.

Ms. DeLuca slung her shoulder bag off with the same weary competence Uncle Donald hung up his game bag after a morning's shooting. Instead of bloodstains, her gear sported a pattern of carousel horses in brown, turquoise, and rust.

"We'll be fine without silverware," she said. "Just bring plenty of bread and some spare napkins. Lemon with the water would be lovely too. No ice."

Ms. DeLuca had thoughtfully waved off Dunstan's cutlery, but he wasn't about to admit a partiality to knives, forks, and spotless ties before opposing counsel.

"And I'd like to see your liquor menu," he said, before Ms. DeLuca excused the wait staff as well. "If it wouldn't be too much bother."

He made the request because good drink was an indulgence available even in the wilds of Maryland, but the greater pleasure was seeing Ms. DeLuca's surprise.

"You drink alcohol during the workday, Mr. Cromarty?"

"You don't? For most of us in solo practice, the workday encompasses lunch and dinner, if not breakfast. A wee dram helps the time pass agreeably."

In the time it took Dunstan to open the menu, Ms. DeLuca castled her mental chess pieces. She clearly did not imbibe during the workday—alas, the Puritans had arrived to these shores in substantial numbers before the Scots—and yet her response was verbal sleight of hand.

"For me, whether to have a drink depends on the selection," she said. "We're close enough to DC that a good wine list isn't rare, but rural enough that it's not a foregone conclusion, either. Now, what shall we have?"

Dunstan knew what he'd have—*anything* as long as it wasn't ruddy chicken or tuna fish—but as he stared at the menu, no particular dish caught his fancy.

He was too busy wondering if, beneath the table, Ms. DeLuca had already divested herself of her ridiculous shoes.

CHAPTER TWO

The Annotated Code of Maryland contained no requirement that an attorney bear personal animosity toward opposing counsel in a lawsuit—just the opposite, in fact. Attorneys were at all times to show civility to parties, witnesses, court personnel, and each other—probably to cranky Scotsmen, too—and yet, Jane was nonplussed to find herself enjoying Dunstan Cromarty's company.

His charm was subtle and easily overlooked, bless his wee Scottish heart.

When Jane walked with him, he did not tear along at a speed intended to broadcast to the world, "I have places to go, people to see, snappy repartee to be overheard exchanging!" as many attorneys did. He sauntered along, because whatever places he had to be or people he had to see, they'd wait for him to arrive.

He'd sauntered along on the *outside*, closest to the street, where an old-fashioned gentleman knew to position himself when escorting a lady. Jane's grandma had probably found that bit of arcana on the Rosetta Stone.

Jane liked that Dunstan Cromarty troubled over his appearance—that suit was *not* JC Pen-wah—though he carried a battle-scarred leather briefcase that looked as if some uncle or grandparent might have passed it down to him.

"I'll have the yesiga sambusa and tikel gomen," Jane said. "With lots of potatoes, and don't spare the bread."

"You'll not be having a salad?" Mr. Cromarty asked. "And am I to order for you, then?"

And there was more of his subtle charm, in the guarded quality of his questions. He was curious, but unwilling to offend, though his manners were probably everything his mama hoped for.

"If you order, then I can start planning dessert. What are you having to drink?"

"They've Fraoch here, a heather ale brewed in Alloa, right along the Firth in Clackmannanshire. Goes with anything, and you don't come across it every day."

That was dessert. That bouquet of Scottish places and terms, served up on a bed of casually rolled r's, enunciated d's, fading g's, and softened vowels.

"Where?"

"Clackmannanshire, up the River Forth from Edinburgh. Very pretty, like most of Scotland. Would you like to try the heather ale?"

Because the rest of the Damson County bar was off planning a Christmas party, the restaurant remained relatively quiet. The few other patrons wandering in wouldn't notice Jane's professional detachment turning to mush at the hope in Dunstan Cromarty's voice.

The man was beer-proud of his homeland. "Why not? Is that where you're from, that Cluck-whatever place?"

He didn't wince, but neither did he approve of her mangling the home of his favored brew.

"Clackmannanshire? No, though my younger brother worked there for a bit. My parents hail from Perth, though my grandparents are all from the west of Scotland."

He put about three extra vowels and a spare syllable in Perth. Paireth. Any juror with ears would be spellbound by that accent, though they might not understand some of what was said—not that juries understood everything they heard, regardless of counsel's accent.

Conversation stalled as the waitress appeared with their water and the bread basket. The scent of the warm, vinegary injera was a pleasure for the nose every bit as delightful as Cromarty's accent was for the ear.

"I'll take that," Jane said, reaching for the bread basket. "And we're ready to order."

Cromarty recalled her selections—even the extra potatoes—and chose shrimp for himself.

"I would have pegged you for a beef kinda guy," she said, peeling off several inches of injera before offering him the basket. "I love this stuff. Love. It. Remember that if you're ever trying to turn me up sweet and there's no decent chocolate on hand."

He accepted the basket and set it down without partaking. "One would never have guessed."

Rather than return fire, Jane savored a bite of sheer, gustatory satisfaction. "Doesn't even need butter, and they always bring lots of it." She hadn't had any injera since Louise had pulled up stakes to teach at an art school.

A family came in with a baby in one of those baby basket-seats, the handle ergonomically twisted to ensure Junior could be hauled about everywhere without Mom or Dad's arm getting tired. This model looked like it came equipped with airbags and an entertainment station.

"There goes the neighborhood," Jane muttered, stuffing another bite of injera into her mouth.

"You don't care for children?"

"I like children a lot, but the rug rat will start bellowing here directly, as soon as Mom and Dad try to have an adult conversation. They're always teething when they're that small."

The little family trundled by, the baby nothing more than a pink, sleepy face among soft blankets and padding.

"The bairnie's too wee to teethe yet," Cromarty said, his tone wistful. He turned a green-eyed gaze on Jane as she inhaled another bite of injera. "I admit to some puzzlement, Ms. DeLuca. You're having bread with your bread and bread with your extra potatoes, and I heard mention of dessert. Are you the only American female who doesn't fret about her weight?"

He posed this question without so much as a hint of a wandering eye, a skill necessary if one was to cross-examine witnesses effectively.

Or hide genuine curiosity.

"I like food, Mr. Cromarty, and though I'm usually careful about what I eat, sometimes a good dose of carby bliss can make an otherwise unpleasant chore bearable. Like your wee dram."

He comprehended the analogy, but—let the record show—did not concede the point. "Is carby a word, then, Ms. DeLuca?"

The baby-family settled in two tables away, and Junior uttered nary a peep.

"There you go being Scottish again. In American, when the punch line is *bliss*, some leeway is allowed with the modifiers."

"For a Scot, when the punch line is *bliss*, no modifiers are necessary. Have you any reason not to send the Almquists to mediation over the custody issues?"

He took the injera in one hand and tore back a strip with the other, the way he might have torn off a strip of paper to jot down his phone number. The gesture was fastidious and gave Jane an entire second to shift from carby-bliss to unpleasant-chore mode.

"Yes, I have a reason for avoiding custody mediation. My guy doesn't want to waste the money. Why spend four hours in court-ordered mediation if you know ahead of time you won't get anywhere?"

"A psychic client. How I wish I'd been retained by one

myself. I don't envy you." He poured his beer into its special beer glass, letting the beer dribble down the side in the exact quantity necessary to form a foamy head without spilling over.

"Not psychic. Broke. Have you talked money with your client?"

"Some. Shall I pour your ale?"

"Please." Because competence in any regard, but especially when it involved a man's hands, was a pleasure. "The Almquists are trying to maintain a decent lifestyle on one income, and mediation could cost them a grand they don't have. Why don't we at least try to come up with a parenting plan for them? They've already parted with the retainers, and they have only the two kids."

He remained silent while he poured Jane's ale, as if putting beer in a glass was his equivalent of savoring carby bliss. When the beer ritual was complete, he passed Jane her drink, then touched his own to it.

"To a quick, equitable, durable settlement."

"Cheers."

She sipped, because that was what the moment called for, and found…designer beer? "This tastes like flowers."

"The heather is infused. The results don't always turn out this well. I'll ask Doreen if she's amenable to a four-way meeting on the subject of parenting and try to come up with some proposals before we meet with you. I take it we're going forward without fault grounds?"

The Toothless Wonder stirred to life. A small fist waved above the batting and blankets, and a thin cry sounded.

"That child wants a beer," Jane said.

"That child wants a cuddle," Cromarty countered, but softly, and as he spoke, the dad extracted the kid from the space shuttle and cradled him against his shoulder. Junior went immediately quiet.

"Do you have children?" Cromarty wore no ring, but— family law, much?—that didn't mean he wasn't a father.

"Cousins, siblings, nieces, nephews." He drew his finger around the rim of his ale glass. "It's in the Almquists' favor that they don't have fault grounds. Their divorce might not be too bad."

Fault grounds, meaning adultery usually. On that cheery thought, the yesiga sambusas were brought to the table. The spicy, meaty scent went surprisingly well with the ale.

"Have one of these," Jane said, holding the plate of sambusas out to him. He was watching the baby, the infant again in charity with the world and grinning over the dad's shoulder. Jane waved the plate a few inches either direction. "Earth to Cromarty, food's here."

That look passed over his features again, a careful non-reaction that pretty much shouted displeasure. In the courtroom, she wouldn't mind putting that look on his face from time to time. Over lunch, however…

"My name is Dunstan, Ms. DeLuca. Dunstan Lachlan Cromarty." He put one of the meat pastries on his plate.

"Is that an invitation to use your first name?" In this enlightened age, Jane did not presume with the guys in any manner she wouldn't want them presuming with her.

And the Laird of Damson County's Family Law Bar probably wouldn't take kindly to presuming from anybody.

Dunstan Lachlan Cromarty unfastened his tie tack—a gold unicorn with a blue gemstone for an eye—and undid a button midway down his shirtfront. Next, he slipped his tie into the gap in his shirt, leaving the button undone, Continental-style.

He looked up when he'd finished rearranging his attire to protect his tie from flying gravy, and the sternness remained in the cast of his features, while in his eye…

A goddamn twinkle?

"How does one put it in American? Me Dunstan, you Jane?"

He bit off a tidy corner of the sambusa, while Jane tried not to choke on her ale. Mr. Cro—*Dunstan*—would be a terror on cross-examination, well prepared, quick, to the point, merciless, and blessed with excellent timing. Poor old Calvin wouldn't know what hit him—again.

But Dunstan Cromarty would be a magnificent terror.

If they went to trial, Jane would just have to be magnificent-er.

They tossed around various parenting scenarios for the Almquists, speculated about the new hire working for Trenton Knightley, and found that heather ale went equally well with shrimp wat and tikel gomen.

As the finger bowls were brought out, and Jane fished around under the table for her shoes, she tried to put a name to what wasn't sitting well.

"This is yours," Dunstan said, passing her her right shoe over to her, then scooting around to reach under the table again. "If you'll give me a moment,"—warm fingers glided over Jane's ankle and shin—"got it."

He passed her the left one.

"My thanks."

While she put her shoes on, he repositioned his tie and tie tack. The moment had an intimate feel, nobody in a hurry, nobody too self-conscious about dealing with wardrobe matters in public, and *that* was also part of what was wrong with the meal.

"I enjoyed this," Jane said as they headed for the register. "Only another lawyer can understand what the practice of law entails, and I like talking shop, and yet, those bar association lunches—"

"We wouldn't be solo practitioners if we craved the constant company of our confreres."

Missing Louise wasn't the same as craving constant company, was it?

Dunstan had his wallet out in a single smooth-guy move. One instant, his hands were empty, the next—bam!—silver plastic was proffered from a worn black billfold.

"We'll split it," Jane said, fishing in her shoulder bag for her wallet. "Or I can get the sambusas because I ordered them."

The lady behind the cash register hesitated before swiping Dunstan's card.

While Jane fumbled around in the depths of a purse-cum-briefcase-cum-gym-bag that Louise had dubbed "The Vast Lonely."

Dunstan leaned closer, close enough that the difference in their sizes became more apparent than usual.

"Jane, cease yer frettin'," he said quietly. "Next time we have a working lunch, you can have the tax deduction."

Jane stopped rummaging in the depths of her shoulder bag, though she did not *cease her frettin'*.

This informal meal between Me Dunstan and You Jane, this experimenting with heather ale and sharing of courthouse gossip, hadn't felt like a working lunch, though some work had been accomplished.

This meal, with Dunstan ordering, Dunstan passing over her shoes, and Dunstan now holding the door for her, had felt like that most rare and precious of all surprises...

An enjoyable date.

***

"I tend to favor mediation," Dunstan said. He'd taken a place across the conference table from his client, the better to protect himself from the aggravation of the scent she wore. "You and Mr. Almquist know your children better than the judge does, you know the family situation better than anybody else, and you are the ones who'll have to live with any parenting schedules included in the court order."

Doreen wore a teal silk blouse—and the teal nails—but her pantsuit was russet, putting Dunstan in mind of... he could not recall what, and it didn't matter, because Doreen had once again accessorized her ensemble with indignation and hurt.

And a baby-powder perfume that made his nose twitch.

"You want us to come up with a parenting schedule," she

said, drumming those nails on the conference table. "If it's parenting, then it's down to me. My yogilates class is full of women who get every other weekend off from the parenting schlepp, and I'd be happy to have that much time to myself."

"The children are in school, aren't they?"

"Subtle, Dunstan." The drumming increased in tempo. "Yes, they're in school, and that means I have little more than six glorious, fun-filled, action-packed hours of the day to do the housework, the yard work, the grocery shopping, the laundry, fit in my classes, get dinner started if I'm doing anything besides leftovers, and handle whatever else that might come my way—I've told Cal for the past year we need to replace that water heater, and lo and behold, yesterday morning was wasted waiting for the delivery guys. And then I put on my chauffeur hat."

"While Calvin does what?"

He asked because she needed to tell this story to somebody, and no real work could be accomplished until she had.

"Hell if I know. He goes down the road each morning, and comes home when he comes home. Traffic on I-270 is the other woman in our marriage when tax season isn't holding him hostage."

"So your parenting proposal is every other weekend with Dad. What about holidays, school breaks, vacations, that sort of thing?"

this was why Dunstan favored mediation, because prodding tired, heartbroken, scared people to think about their children, about how the divorce would affect those helpless to prevent it, was in itself wearying and heartbreaking.

His lower back agreed, so he got up and adjusted the blinds in his small conference room.

"The boys gave up on Cal years ago," Doreen said. Around the conference room, Dunstan had hung poster-size sticky notes, a twenty-eight-square grid marked out on each one in black. The squares were filled with red M's and green D's, for

Mom and Dad. "And I'm not a dad, Dunstan."

The sight of those damned squares never failed to bother Dunstan. "What if you had a different schedule for tax season and the rest of the year? Mightn't Calvin find more time for his children?"

Her nails stopped drumming for the space of three quiet seconds, then resumed. "He's scared of those boys. They're loud, they're messy, they forget to put the seat down, and they're interested in girls."

"They have something in common with their father, then," Dunstan said, resuming his place at the table to copy the schedules on the wall onto his legal pad.

"Gonads? Gorillas have those. I hear more about junk, packages, and—if it weren't for the Dictionary of Urban Slang, I'd hardly know when to scold my own sons."

And yet, she didn't make the effort to talk to her husband, or had given up trying, and refused counseling. Dunstan was reminded of the quote about happy families being all the same, but troubled ones each having their own tale or woe.

Which thought was interrupted by a prodigious sneeze, followed by a terse "bless you" from Doreen.

Dunstan tended to pinch his nose together when he sneezed, which his mother claimed would cause his eyeballs to explode, though it saved him the great honk of an escaped sneeze. He put his handkerchief to use and scooted his chair back.

"Think about parenting options you can offer your husband, Doreen, the more the better. We're brainstorming now, trying to be creative. I've been looking at your budget, and at the statement of assets and liabilities. You should still consider counseling. Single parenting is hard, even harder than the parenting you're doing now."

She rose swiftly. "Counseling costs money when we're broke enough as it is. I'm not good at numbers. That's why I married an accountant."

And if Calvin thought he was valued only for his accounting, how was he to know the missus was longing for a family picnic or wild, monkey, laundry room sex?

"Money is always a delicate topic when a marriage ends. How do you and Calvin manage it?"

While Doreen wandered around the room studying the various schedules as if they were displays in some contemporary art gallery, Dunstan cracked the window and drew from her a picture of family finances as rigid and distant as the parties themselves.

"So you pay all the household bills from the account in your name, while Calvin manages the investments?"

"I don't understand all that SEP, T-whatever stuff, and Cal thrives on it. He puts a chunk of cash in the household account, and I pay the bills. That way, he doesn't bother me about every little carryout order or heating bill. It's one part of our marriage that hasn't caused problems yet."

She was either ashamed, lying, trying not to cry, perhaps all three.

"If you can have only one part of the marriage functioning smoothly, finances are a good one to have. What does Calvin do for spending money?"

Doreen paused before the window, which looked out over a long, narrow backyard, the office being a renovated row house a block away from the courthouse.

"That is a beautiful oak, out behind your office."

The tree was huge, probably centuries old, and at present a luminous yellow in its autumn plumage. The weather was changing, though, the temperature dropping, the wind tearing at the leaves remaining on the branches. Then too, the increasing chill had turned Dunstan's back twinge-y again.

"Aye, it's pretty, but those falling leaves clog every gutter and downspout for half a block. You were telling me about Calvin's spending money." Or she was avoiding talking about it, though she could linger by the window all morning if it would spare Dunstan another sneeze.

"He has his own credit card, probably one of those business cards in some impressive, glossy finish. I don't bother him over it. All he does is buy gas with it unless he's off to some accounting conference."

Uncle Donald claimed that hunting had less to do with good aim and more to do with the ability to sit still and shut up. Game wandered into view sooner or later, if the hunter could be patient.

"We'll need to have a look at *all* the bank statements, Doreen. *Every* bill, *every* credit card statement. Calvin is an accountant, he'll understand why verification is needed for what's on the accounting filed at the courthouse."

She put her hand on the window glass, her teal nails spread against a backdrop of golden oak leaves soon to fall. "He'll fuss. Is that really necessary?"

Dunstan stayed where he was, enduring a pang of sympathy for Doreen Almquist while an eddy of chilly autumn air rescued him from another sneeze. She was disappointed in Calvin—or disappointed in life and attributing more than a fair share to her husband—but she believed Calvin was a basically decent fellow she was no longer attracted to.

"Calvin is a CPA, Doreen, and he's keeping a separate account you never see, and though most men in his position would expect to handle the household bills, he's turned that over entirely to you, and he never—not at Christmas or birthdays, not for the yard work or the new water heater— double-checks your work or second-guesses your decisions. That makes me nervous."

She pushed away from the window and retrieved a shimmery, silky, taupe overcoat from the coat rack in the corner. That coat was pretty and likely felt lovely on, but it wouldn't keep her warm when the weather changed, which this time of year was inevitable.

"Good," she said. "I'm paying you to know when to be

nervous. I'll meet you here at nine thirty Tuesday morning and go over my parenting proposals with you before Calvin and his lawyer arrive."

"Until Tuesday," he said, getting to his feet. "And please compile copies of the household bills and bank statements, Doreen. The parenting schedule might be easy, but the money could get interesting."

She paused, a taupe silk scarf hanging around her neck, her coat gaping open.

"It's called rehabilitative alimony, right? So I can get back to work, complete a master's degree, maybe get a PhD. A fine idea, but who's going to finish raising our children while I'm recovering from fourteen years of stay-home parenting and Calvin's sitting in traffic?"

She whipped the scarf over her shoulder and swept out, a woman entitled to her petty dramas and parting shots.

But Dunstan prayed to God he'd sniffed the last of whatever fragrance she'd worn today. Most perfumes didn't bother him—and some, say, that favored by Jane DeLuca—he liked—but if Doreen wore the baby powder scent again, he'd have to say something.

And the tickle in his nose was accompanied by a tickle in his memory. Teal was close to turquoise, and Dunstan's mind clicked into recognition: Doreen's wardrobe favored the same colors as Jane DeLuca's carpetbag, though carousel horses and angry housewives were very different uses of the same hues.

He pushed aside his recollection of Jane rummaging in her bag as she tried desperately to prevent him from paying for her meal. Tried and failed.

No more cozy lunches with opposing counsel for him, not when the Almquist case was developing a faint odor of complication and bad behavior.

Doreen maintained her designer wardrobe, designer nails, designer hair, and designer body out of the household account, while also driving an SUV that likely averaged twelve miles to the gallon and four entertainment stations per child.

Spin classes, yoga classes, lunch with the ladies, membership at the bath and tennis club if not the country club… All of that cost money, and Calvin managed to provide for it on an accountant's salary, while also contributing to investment and retirement assets.

Dunstan left the sticky posters where they were, for by this time Tuesday, those draft schedules would sport every color of the rainbow. Despite all the discussion and worry that went into the final product, Calvin would likely end up with every other weekend, alternating holidays, and two non-consecutive weeks in the summer.

Unless he was serving time in a federal prison for embezzlement or fraud.

***

Dunstan Cromarty's office was almost what Jane had expected: a *historical* row house, renovated in the nick of time for office use, complete with narrow stairs, creaking floors, and chair rails bearing at least a century's worth of nicks and dents.

The octagonal conference table, however, was magnificent.

"I wonder how many hours Cromarty billed to be able to afford this table," Calvin said, taking a seat. "Maybe I should carve my initials into it for my contribution."

"Don't be sacrilegious," Jane retorted, stroking the rich, red-blond surface of the table. "Chestnut trees in Maryland all but died out when the chestnut blight came through a century ago. My grandpapa said antiques like this are all that remain of a gorgeous and once-thriving native tree."

"That's not exactly true."

Dunstan Cromarty stood in the doorway to the conference room, his suit today a dark, forest-at-sunset green, his tie a paisley in shades much like the polished wood of the table. Tie tack and cuff links matched again, gold with inset amber—a lion this time, not a fanciful unicorn.

He wore wire-rimmed glasses halfway down his nose that, for reasons Jane would examine in solitude, made her wonder what he'd look like wearing *only* those glasses.

"Mr. Cromarty." She rose and extended a hand, because demonstrating to the clients that matters would proceed civilly—*not* speculating about opposing counsel's physique—was the first order of business. "I'd like to introduce Mr. Calvin Almquist. Calvin, Dunstan Cromarty."

They shook, Calvin eyeing Dunstan like a frat boy pledging a rival house.

"Mrs. Almquist and I will join you shortly," Dunstan said. "Can I get anybody a cup of coffee?"

More civilities, of course, though it would be law office coffee, which only night-shift cops or nurses would regard as drinkable. Jane demurred and resumed her seat when Dunstan had withdrawn to whatever neutral corner his client lurked in.

"Is making us wait in here supposed to be a tactic?" Calvin asked, thumping his metal briefcase onto the conference table with about as much regard for the finish as a dog had for the sofa's upholstery.

"We were a little early, Cal. That wasn't a tactic on our part, so no, I won't start accusing anybody of tactics yet." Nor would she speculate any further on whether—twice—Dunstan had touched her foot by accident or by design.

And if by design, had he been trying to distract her from the case?

Mrs. Almquist was like Dunstan's office. In general, she was pretty much as expected: mid-to-late thirties, chilly, wary, tired, and dreading what lay between her and her freedom. She was a bit unexpected too, though, in that she was well put together, right down to lacquered bronze nails, honey-blond highlights, sculpted brows, expert makeup, and a blue silk suit that tactfully whispered outstanding good taste.

She hadn't let herself go to pot. Just the opposite, right down to a light, baby powder and freesia scent.

Calvin didn't stand when his wife came in, and neither did Mrs. Almquist offer her ex-to-be any greeting.

Dunstan shot Jane a single, veiled glance: *Let the wild rumpus begin.*

Under the table, Jane toed off her ballet flats and prepared to model sweet reason and professional cooperation for the Almquists.

"Ms. DeLuca and I thought we'd use today's meeting to consider parenting schedules," Dunstan said, "but if we can't come up with something you both agree to, then Maryland law pretty much requires that you attempt mediation."

Calvin popped the latches on his briefcase. "You mean we have to pay for both? For you two spinning your wheels and then some touchy-feely counselor type wasting more of our time? Thanks so much. If we take long enough to figure out how I'm to become a stranger to my own children, then we won't have to worry about paying for their college educations, because I'll be too broke."

Doreen slapped both palms onto the table. "You're already a stranger to them, though they're *our* children. The point of this divorce is to ensure you become a stranger to me too. Nobody told you to go for the partner slot, Cal. That was your decision."

"Children cost money, Dorie."

Some attorneys would have let this venting and posturing go on until the clients ran out of steam, but Jane had already had enough.

"Your bickering costs money too, at least when Mr. Cromarty and I are in the room. You can stand out in the parking lot all afternoon berating each other, but today we're supposed to focus on your children. How are they doing?"

Playing the kid card so early was a calculated risk, but this time, it paid off. Husband and wife exchanged sad, guilty looks.

"Mark asked me if I was moving to DC," Calvin said. "He was giving me permission—my own son, *giving me permission*—

to abandon him. Luke won't say anything, but…"

But a child's silences could bludgeon even an absent parent.

Dunstan pushed his glasses up his nose and passed over several pieces of paper. "Mrs. Almquist and I came up with this schedule for tax season, which we understand to be Mr. Almquist's busiest time. We're hoping that over the summer, the boys can spend more time with their father."

"So I get them when I'll have to take off work to look after them?" Calvin said, wrinkling his nose. "Or I can put them in hockey camp all summer, and forget about affording any vacations."

For the next hour, it went like that. Every attempt at concession from one spouse met with suspicion and grumbling from the other. One would indulge in a flare of temper while the other tried for compromise, then the roles would switch. Jane intervened when her own client was particularly nasty, Dunstan reined in Mrs. Almquist when she was similarly uncooperative.

Dunstan was inclined to roam the room, and at one point he cracked the conference room door a few inches for no reason Jane could discern, because the room was neither warm nor cold.

They eventually wrangled a basic schedule into place, though both parties would take the next week to consider the tentative agreement.

"I'll make copies of these," Dunstan said, collecting the most recent version of the four-week parenting pattern. "Doreen, if you'd join me for a moment?"

"What are they talking about?" Calvin asked, though the question had none of his previous snark. Putting down on paper the reality of a family splitting apart would wallop the snark out of anybody.

"If the parenting agreement flies, then the next step is usually the division of marital assets, but I have a question for you, Calvin."

"I'm apparently full of answers today. I've never seen Dorie so subdued."

And this bothered him, which was the price extracted from a man who *could* pay attention to his wife, but hadn't for too long.

"For many couples, the parenting aspect of the divorce is the worst part. Once they know they'll still be able to spend time with their children, they can pay attention to the rest of the agenda more easily. Any time you want to put the divorce on pause and try some counseling with Doreen, you let me know."

At some point, Calvin's international document courier briefcase had found its way to the floor. He set it back on the table now as if it were a cinder block, not an essentially empty box.

"Doreen would never go to counseling, and there's no easy part to ripping your life in two. We'll get through the money issues, but I don't see how we'll hang on to that house. Dorie loves that house, and the boys have friends all over the neighborhood."

"That was sort of what I wanted to ask you. Doreen takes good care of herself."

He rummaged in his briefcase. "She does—tennis, spin classes, yoga, zumba, swimming, massages, and that sort of thing. Always has and has insisted I do likewise. She's right. A lot of the guys at the office are not exactly fit—accounting is a sedentary profession—but Dorie says if we don't want the kids to sit around playing video games all day, we need to get off our duffs too."

"You should thank her for that." *In counseling.*

Calvin closed the briefcase, crossed his arms on top of it, and rested his forehead on his wrists. "Then she'll snap at me, tell me if I could listen to her about staying fit, then why not about anything else? I'll snap back that nobody wants to listen to constant bitching…" He heaved a sigh and straightened.

"What did you want to ask?"

"How does she afford all that upkeep? She's sporting salon nails, salon hair, and that was a lovely outfit. The shoes were either very good Jimmy Choo knock-offs or the real deal, and her handbag—" Would have paid for several counseling sessions by itself.

"I don't know this Choo guy, but Doreen manages on what I put in the household account. I suppose that will change."

Everything would change, everything except the leaden feeling old Cal drove up and down the interstate with each day, and that would hang around all too faithfully.

"All of those classes and memberships cost money, Cal. I'll bet she has her hair done down in DC and shops for her clothes at least at White Flint. Mr. Choo doesn't get out this way much. Do you typically give Doreen jewelry for birthdays and Christmas?"

He gazed off into the middle distance, an emotionally overwhelmed and exhausted man trying to make his intellect function. "Not jewelry. Dorie buys that herself—she has better taste than I ever will. I'll send her flowers, or stuff that can be planted."

Dorie had been wearing four rings—in addition to her wedding rings, interestingly—each sporting a semi-precious stone in a craftsman setting, as well as bracelets and earrings to match.

"Her household account will bear some scrutiny," Jane said, discreetly toeing her right ballet flat back onto her foot. "Maybe she clips a lot of coupons, maybe she's a secret shopper, but nobody looks that well put together for nothing."

"She smells good too," Calvin said wistfully, now that nobody of any import could overhear him. "Even when she comes home from the gym, that woman smells good and has every day I've known her. The boys will have to do some looking to find wives who measure up to the standard Doreen has set."

Ah, the sentimentality of the soon-to-be single.

"Maintaining that standard when you're trying to establish a second household will be a challenge, Cal, and I can promise you Doreen will not meet that challenge graciously."

Jane maneuvered the left ballet flat on and stood. "I can send you the notes if you want to be on your way. The weather's supposed to get stinky this afternoon, and the temperature has already started to drop. You might want get going before the drizzle starts freezing. Mr. Cromarty and I will probably need some time to confer anyway."

"About?"

Calvin was not a trusting soul, but that was to be expected when his wife of seventeen years had turned into a stranger, and his children could well do likewise.

"Who's to draft the parenting agreement, when will he have Doreen's version of the financial statement together, when will I have yours? This stagecoach doesn't drive itself, but you're off to a good start."

Sort of like congratulating somebody on putting together an excellent funeral.

He checked his watch, a big, clunky, fourteen-function deal held to his wrist with the jeweler's equivalent of a chain-link fence. Nobody wore a watch any more, cell phones serving the need more than adequately, but Calvin probably relished the comfort of a dedicated timepiece that doubled as an altimeter and food processor.

"I'm off to the salt mines, then. At least this time of day, traffic will be light."

"You ever think of telecommuting one or two days a week in the off-season?"

Jane telecommuted frequently when she didn't have to be in court. Put on her best bathrobe and most comfy slippers, popped open her laptop, and alternated drafting legal motions with Spider Solitaire marathons all from the comfort of her favorite corner of the sofa.

Nothing like a seemingly impossible game of Spider for helping the subconscious tackle sticky legal puzzles.

"One of the partners telecommutes," Cal said, shrugging into a Burberry raincoat. "She lives on the other side of Baltimore. The gas and commuting time made the argument for her, though during tax season, it's all hands on deck, no matter where you live."

On that naval note, he departed for his rainy commute.

CHAPTER THREE

Anybody handling divorce work needed to acquaint themselves with the traditional phases of grieving: denial, anger, bargaining, depression, and acceptance. Clients ricocheted through them, sometimes touching four out of five in the space of ten minutes.

The fifth phase…acceptance. That one was elusive. Dunstan sensed the Almquists might never attain it.

"Don't look out the window," Jane DeLuca said, stuffing her undersized computer into her oversized carpetbag. "Our clients are not at their best."

"One doesn't expect them to be," Dunstan said, passing over copies of the first-round parenting schedule. He, of course, took a gander out the window so he could surreptitiously open it another three inches and begin detoxing the baby powder nerve gas from the room. "Oh, for God's sake."

"I warned you," Jane said, coming to stand beside him. "Pathetic, but predictable. I've tried to nudge Cal into counseling, but he's the white knuckle divorce type, apparently."

Under the old oak, dead leaves drifting around them, rain mizzling down, Calvin held Doreen and stroked her hair. Mrs. Almquist was clearly in tears, and Calvin…

"Your client is pretty broken up about this divorce,"

Dunstan said, knowing he should look away, but enjoying a moment with opposing counsel standing next to him, despite the sad tableau under the oak *and* the tickle in his sinuses. "Hit him by surprise."

And that wasn't what Dunstan had expected. Embezzlers were a canny lot, usually. The cheeriest people you'd ever want to meet, all the while sliding a hand into your pocket.

"They seem like a good team," Jane said. "I get that violent relationships need to end, but for people like these, I can't fathom what is so awful, what is so damned, unbearably miserable, that signing up for Match.com looks good in comparison to what you've spent years building with your children's other parent."

"One of life's great mysteries. My Uncle Donald says if birds can mate for life, great apes ought to be able to pull it off."

"What does your aunt say?"

"Uncle isna married." Though he had close and abiding relationships with his pocket flask and his weaponry.

"Dunstan, may I ask you something?"

And here it came, the sticky, tricky question, about foregoing court-ordered discovery on the financial documents, or about sending the clients for financial mediation, where such informality was often the norm.

"Aye, but let's move away from the window."

For the Almquists were having a good, long, miserable cuddle amid the dead leaves and autumn mist.

"I don't begrudge them a moment to console each other," Jane said, stuffing the schedule into the depths of her carpetbag. "But too much of that, and they'll turn their gun sights on us."

Because whatever animosity the divorce engendered often did end up being aimed at *the lawyers*, giving parties desperate for common ground targets they could both fire at.

"They'll get around to playing get-the-lawyers eventually

anyhow," Dunstan said, closing the curtain over the window. Which was a…mistake. The day was dreary, and closing the curtains cast the small conference room into a cozy gloom, like a confessional. "If you're about to ask about waiving formal discovery, I haven't discussed the notion with my client."

Nor would he. Waiving formal discovery, where the court oversaw the fact-finding phase of the case, was ill-advised.

"Discovery shouldn't be a problem," Jane said, zipping her carpetbag closed. "I get the sense your client has control of all the household accounts and bills, so most of the documentation should come from her."

"You're shorter today. Shorter than usual." He liked that, though he also liked how she prowled around in her spiky heels, a family law superheroine in pursuit of any villains bent on world domination.

"I'm short every day." She plucked Dunstan's glasses from his nose and handed them to him. "Are these for show, or do you really need them? Glasses make a great courtroom prop. I wore flats because it's raining, or sleeting, or something."

She scooted onto the conference table and kicked out a foot with a slipper-looking black shoe on it.

Dunstan busied himself tidying papers into no particular order rather than examine her feet. He'd touched her ankle bones, found them slim and sharp, her calf sturdy, and—

He needed to get out more, and not to the Knightley brothers' poker nights. "Sensible of you, I'm sure, to forego the heels. When do you expect to file your motions for discovery?"

"In the library the other day, and at the restaurant, did you touch my—touch *me* on purpose?"

The question was oh-so-casual and completely unexpected, as the best cross-examination could be. A world of possibilities lay in that question, most of them bad.

"If I say yes, you'll have me up before the bar association for sexual harassment, sent off to naughty-lawyer classes and begging to keep my license, or at the very least, you'll move to kick me off this case."

She might also charge him with assault for the hell of it, assault being any harmful or offensive touching. The state's attorney was a right bastard who'd delight in handling the case too.

No sense of humor at the prosecutor's office, though the first time, in the library, Dunstan hadn't entirely intended to take liberties.

And Dunstan hadn't earned nearly enough of the Almquist retainer. Then too, if Jane knew her client's hands were financially dirty, forcing Mrs. Almquist to change lawyers would obscure that difficult reality nicely.

A wonderful legal analysis of the facts, far too late to do him any good.

"James Knightley claims you meet some very nice people in naughty-lawyer classes," Jane said, scooting off the conference table. "Not that he's attended."

James Knightley was damned good-looking, also shrewd. He was the local expert on corporate law, which meant he could—and did—date the entire rest of the

Damson County Women's Bar Association with little chance of a conflict of interest.

"Let me ask you a question, then, Counselor," Dunstan said. He unhooked Jane's raincoat from the rack and held it open for her. "Was your wee foot trying to evade my hand? On either occasion?"

Because another hypothesis could explain why she'd bring this up now:

Jane DeLuca, spikey-heeled terror of the Damson County family law bar, needed to get out more too.

***

Dunstan Cromarty had the knack of holding a lady's coat so she didn't have to contort herself into it, but could instead stand more or less passively while her outerwear was slipped up her arms and draped over her shoulders.

The sensation was…lovely and novel, and that Jane allowed this courtesy probably answered any questions about her *wee fute* and whether she'd complain to the bar association about a moment or two of slap and tickle.

"Dunstan, where's your staff?" Jane asked, because she and opposing counsel were apparently to have a somewhat awkward conversation about boundaries and professionalism.

About which her feet were not happy at all.

"My staff is larking about Lancaster County on some quilt tour. They asked for the day off weeks ago, and I usually manage well enough without them. My paralegal's only half time, and my secretary leaves at three thirty to pick up her kids."

Knowing he was a good boss did nothing to help Jane maintain a professional distance. "Why aren't you in Scotland, Cromarty?"

"I often think of going home, but I won't do that until my coffers will allow a successful transition to practice there. When you're a solo practitioner, and all the overhead falls to you, you make little financial headway."

He said this standing behind Jane, as if he didn't want her to see him admit homesickness, or the weariness that came with being a solo practitioner.

"Tell me about it," Jane said, stepping away. She cracked the curtain over the window and saw the Almquists giving each other a final hug beside a blue SUV, Cal's briefcase at his feet, his hand braced near his wife's shoulder.

"Jane, about your question?"

She could tell by his tone that the awkward discussion would be blessedly brief. He'd meant nothing, he hadn't been flirting, it wouldn't happen again. No harm, no foul.

No more lunches without cutlery, no more speculating about what Dunstan Cromarty looked like wearing only his glasses.

"You have very pretty feet," he said, which was an interesting opening statement, but whatever else he might have said was lost in a great sneeze that he silenced by pinching his nose closed.

"Didn't your mother tell you not to do that?" Jane asked, shouldering her carpetbag. "You're supposed to let a sneeze out, not trap it, because it can do all kinds of—Dunstan? Cromarty?"

He stood bent forward a few peculiar inches at the waist, one hand braced on the conference table. His expression had a listening quality, like a juvenile delinquent who'd just knocked back a fifth of Jim Beam might listen for the approach of sirens—or death.

Jane set her bag on the table. "Dunstan, is something wrong? You've gone pale."

Even his lips were pale, and his eyes suggested his innocent client had just been given twenty to life.

"Are you having a heart attack?"

He eased out a breath. "Nay. Not a heart attack. It's m' back." He commenced to swearing softly, carefully, such as a man does when even breathing too deeply promises crippling pain.

Jane caught a few "fookin's," a "shite," and some other words that were too heavily accented for her to make out.

"Do we need to get you to urgent care?"

Because she was alone with him—drat and damn all quilt tours—and she couldn't leave him like this. Fortunately, she had neither court nor client appointments for the rest of the day, though she had work aplenty.

"I'll be fine. Some heat, some rest, a wee dram or two, and I'll come right. I always have before. You can run along now."

He hadn't moved, hadn't shifted his posture a single millimeter.

"*Run along*? And leave you the oil can? You won't be that lucky. I let you pay for lunch, you'll let me drive you home."

He wanted to argue. Jane could see the words fighting to get past his white lips, could see pride and pragmatism having a badass rumble, with common sense holding all bets.

"I'll get your briefcase," she said. "What else do you need?"

"I'll be—"

"You'll be laid up for a couple days, but if you tell me which files to grab, you can at least stare at them until the wee drams work their magic. If you argue with me on this, I'll tickle you."

"Shameless tactics," he muttered, as he began a slow, shuffling, half-bent progress toward the door. "The Almquist file will do. Throw in the Fosters' agreement too—that one's on my desk. Grab Baxter while you're about it, and maybe Ostergard, as well."

"You're taking a couple days at home, Dunstan, not setting up a home office. Where are your keys?"

Progress to the parking lot was slow and silent, with Jane carrying both her carpetbag and Dunstan's battered briefcase.

"I'll not be able to get out of that," Dunstan said as they approached Jane's powder-blue Prius. "And gettin' in won't be a treat, either."

While she sympathized with his misery, Jane had rather enjoyed his bad language. "What do you propose?"

"My vehicle will do."

His vehicle. The small parking lot held three other cars, all with a dusting of wet, yellow oak leaves and the occasional oversized snowflake. "The Camry?"

"The Tundra."

A Tundra was a…truck. A big, muddy black truck with the tailgate down and testosterone tires such as Jane could have neither lifted nor afforded. "You can get into that thing?"

"I'll haul myself up by the handles. You'll have to drive."

First, she had to wait as Dunstan by groans and inches shifted himself up into the passenger's seat. He settled back slowly, slowly, never seeming to reach a place of comfort. Jane slammed his door closed and came around to the driver's side.

Getting in was undignified, and the seat was way too far back, but the view was lovely.

"I've always wanted to drive a truck," she said, fitting the key into the ignition and cranking the engine. "I like sitting up this high, and these seats are cushy. Is this the seat heater?"

She hit two buttons, cranking his up to high and putting her own at medium. Everything on the dash was fairly self-explanatory, and the truck steered beautifully.

So it was completely by accident that Jane bumped a rear wheel over a curb pulling out, causing Dunstan to curse for nearly half a block in a language she didn't recognize.

***

Please, Almighty Merciful God, do not let Wallace be playing turd hockey on the kitchen floor when I hobble in the door with Jane DeLuca at my side.

"You haven't passed out on me, have you?" Jane asked as she shut the truck off. "Your eyes are closed."

"I'm gathering my strength." For any number of ordeals.

"Don't you move until I've rappelled down the cliff side," she said, scrambling out of the driver's seat.

She was so little, she had to more or less jump out of the truck, while Dunstan… He moved one leg, then the other. He paused to let the agony bounce around in his body, then used the handles to haul himself sideways, and so it went, one indignity, one torment at a time.

Jane shouldered their various bags, while Dunstan caught sight of Wallace sitting in the living room window, a marmalade ball of gloating feline.

"Oh, you have a kitty! What's his name?"

"Fat Bastard. The door's nae locked."

She opened the door and stood back so Dunstan could totter past her, then she hauled their bags in and closed the door. "Is an unlocked door prudent? You're fairly isolated here."

"I'm hoping somebody will come by and steal the cat." Who, in an unprecedented display of survival instinct, had neither recently used the litter box, nor undertaken any hockey games that Dunstan could see.

It being a hallmark of Wallace's hockey seasons that cat litter was sprinkled from one end of the downstairs to the other.

"I love these old farm houses," Jane said, shrugging out of her coat. "They have charm."

Dunstan stretched out a casual hand and braced himself against the nearest wall, a compromise between his tattered dignity and the urge to crumple in a screaming fetal heap three steps inside the door.

"These old farm houses have heating bills. If you'd like to take my truck back to town, I can have one of the Knightleys give me a lift tomorrow."

He didn't attempt a smile, neither did he try to get to the sofa, a good five yards, three cursing fits, and four prayers off across the living room. Carpeted yards, though, which would make crawling ever so much more comfy.

"I'm not going anywhere," Jane said, and damn the woman, she spoke with the patient amusement of a small female with a perfectly functional sacroiliac. "The first order of business should be to get you into a hot shower, if your bad back is anything like my grandpa's. Is your bedroom upstairs?"

"I'll be adorning the sofa for a wee bit before attempting anything so ambitious as a shower." Though a shower…His muscles stopped pounding on his tailbone long enough to beg for that hot shower even before he opened his last bottle of twenty-five-year-old Glenmorangie single malt.

"So you can't make it up the stairs. Does this level have a bathroom?"

He didn't like this line of questioning one bit. "Aye."

"Then what are you waiting for?"

Disaster for Scotland, to put the situation mildly. "I'm

waiting for the floor to open up and swallow me whole. I'll not allow you to undress me, Jane DeLuca."

Not like this, please God. Not like this.

"So we'll put you in the shower with your clothes on. Would you leave me to suffer when my back hurt so badly I couldn't stand the thought of sneezing again?"

He crossed himself with the hand that wasn't anchored to the wall. "You're a cruel woman to mention such a thing. There'll be no sneezing of any kind for the foreseeable future."

And not to put too fine a point on it, his diet would be rich in fiber, once he could stand in the kitchen long enough to pour milk on cereal. Wallace chose then to strop himself across Dunstan's legs.

"He knows I canna kick him."

Jane inserted herself under Dunstan's outstretched arm, which was about three seconds away from shaking. "Lean on me. Anybody who names a cat Fat Bastard has already abused the animal. I assume the facilities are down the hall?"

Miles away, of course. Why didn't old farm houses have bathrooms in the foyer?

"Second door on the left."

He tried not to lean on her—and failed. Jane was surprisingly sturdy, though, and they covered the distance to the bathroom with only a bit more swearing. Then she abandoned him— abandoned him—with an admonition to get off as much of his clothing as he could while she retrieved sweats from his bedroom upstairs.

Sometimes, when his back went out, within twenty minutes, he could tell he was due for only a light penance. A dose of painkiller, time lying prone, a movie or two, and all could be forgiven, provided he took no chances for several days.

This was shaping up to be a less accommodating episode.

Dunstan undressed in the bathroom, his clothes piled into a heap at his feet, for he could not bend down to hang them up and couldn't balance on one foot long enough to hook them with his toes—he knew all the tricks. He could manage to brush his teeth and tend to other standing rituals, and by the time he heard a tap on the door, he was sporting only a towel about his hips.

"It's nae locked."

"Good," Jane said, pushing the door closed behind her. "I found sweats, but wouldn't a kilt be easier? You don't have to step into it."

She brandished a black work kilt Dunstan wore when waging his endless war with the yard.

"That's a fetching ensemble you're wearing yourself, Ms. DeLuca." For she'd changed into gray sweats and a green T-shirt that said *If it takes three years to get there, it had better be one helluva bar*.

"I always have gym clothes with me," she said, turning on the bathtub taps and holding her hand under the gushing stream.

Maybe she frequently found herself sleeping in places other than her own bed? Not a cheering thought.

She fiddled with the taps, and soon, water streamed from the shower head in steamy abundance. The difficulty before Dunstan daunted him: He had to raise each foot high enough to step into the shower and shift his weight without falling.

"In you go," Jane said, showing no indication of absenting herself. "If you think I'll let you risk a slip-and-fall now, you're dumber than I thought." She stepped closer and put her arms around Dunstan's bare torso. "Lean on me, and no heroic measures, because I'll probably topple with you, and I will sue you if I injure anything other than my pride."

He leaned, he tottered, he leaned some more, and finally, finally, found his way to the soothing, hot spray. Jane whisked his towel off and flipped the Royal Stewart plaid shower curtain closed in the same nanosecond, but the bliss of the hot water was so great, Dunstan almost didn't care what she saw, or what she thought of what she saw.

Almost.

***

Jane hadn't looked, truly she hadn't, but she'd *seen* anyway.

She paused outside the bathroom door, back braced against the wall as images of a naked Dunstan Cromarty danced through her head—and a few points south.

A long, tapered back that flowed into a taut, male tush; defined musculature on every limb; the proverbial washboard abs; and a chest that really deserved to be immortalized on the covers of a few romance novels.

And as for the rest...

She contemplated the rest of him, *at length*, as it were, until the shower stopped. In the ensuing silence, reason rescued Jane from considering career suicide: Dunstan Cromarty wasn't interested in her. That's what his *pretty fute* speech would have been about, had he been allowed to finish it.

"Do not even think of getting out of that shower, Dunstan Cromarty," Jane called, as she opened the bathroom door. Fragrant steam beclouded her senses, along with the knowledge that a big, wet, hurting Scot stood on the other side of the shower curtain.

"Pass me the towel, Jane, or I'll scandalize us both."

Let the scandalizing begin. "This one's dry." She slid a fluffy red bath towel around the end of the shower curtain. "Towel off as best you can, and then I'll pass you the kilt."

He didn't manscape. He probably didn't even know what manscaping was, and Jane hoped he never learned.

"I'll have that kilt now."

The damp towel was thrust forth. Jane made the swap. "Do you feel any better?"

"Aye, a bit. I'll break out the heating pad, take a few pills, and settle in for the rest of the day. This will pass."

Jane leaned against the wall, trying not to picture Dunstan Cromarty fastening on a kilt. "Do you have court tomorrow?"

"Nay, thank Christ. I wouldna answer for the consequences

if I had to listen to Elvin Gregory's bleating when my back's troubling me. No court until next week. You?"

"Same. Shall we get you out of there?"

The shower curtain whipped back, revealing a damp Dunstan Cromarty wearing nothing but a pleated black kilt and a scowl. "I can manage."

"I can help." He hated this, hated being seen helpless, and Jane could understand that. "My Aunt Della fell in the shower and busted a hip. She lay there for more than a day before my cousin found her."

A heavy arm settled across Jane's shoulders. "You're such a ray of sunshine, wee Jane. How have I functioned without you in my bathroom all these years? In case you haven't noticed, I'm not your auld auntie."

"One foot at a time," Jane said, tucking an arm around his waist.

He moved somewhat more easily, so Jane let him find his way to the couch on his own and tidied up in the bathroom. She left the door open to let the steam out, tossed the dirties and the used towels in a closet washing machine and started the load.

"Where's the heating pad?"

"In the linen closet upstairs, but you mustn't let the cat see you plugging it in."

"I noticed cat food in a plastic container labeled 'Wallace.' Do you have more than one cat?"

Dunstan eased back on the sofa cushions, and carefully, carefully, stretched out full length. "His proper name is Fat Bastard Wallace Cromarty. The whiskey's above the cat food in the pantry. Perhaps you'll share a dram with me?"

The Scots were reputed to be a hospitable lot, unless they were planning murder or treason—much like the Italians. Jane went off in search of hooch and a heating pad.

Dunstan's house was tidy, even his king-size bed was made—cozy Black Watch plaid flannel sheets and wool blankets—and his personal bathroom was spotless. Sheets and towels in the linen closet were neatly folded and stacked, lavender soaps and sachets tucked between them.

And yet, two spare rooms down the hall from his bedroom were empty. Not sparsely furnished, but echoingly empty. No curtains, no stacked boxes.

The pantry shelves presented the same picture: What stores Dunstan had—healthy cereal, canned soup (low salt, not low fat), tea, coffee, a bag of gourmet bite-size dark chocolates— were arranged for easy access, but more than half the shelves were empty.

And only one box of pasta, one can of tomato sauce, one can of chili beans, though again, the quality was good.

"Why do you stock your larder like an old person?" Jane asked as she plugged in the heating pad.

"Now you've done it. Wallace and that heating pad have an unnatural relationship."

The heating pad's flannel sleeve was Black Watch plaid. Wallace hopped down from the upright piano and positioned himself sphinx-like on the arm of the sofa.

"He heard you summon him," Jane said, though the cat's dimensions suggested an open can of fancy white albacore was the only summons he truly heeded. "Scoot a bit."

Dunstan snatched the heating pad from her rather than allow her to tuck it behind him. "I'll do it."

He positioned it low against his back—very low.

"You have two empty rooms upstairs," Jane said. "Is that Scottish frugality, or a sign of impending departure for the Auld Sod?"

Because somewhere in the *Lonely Woman's Handbook of Heartbreak*, it was written that just as that woman finally found a man who might—*might*—interest her, he had to ship out for his next assignment, transfer to the home office, or otherwise become geographically compromised.

Though Jane was not interested in Dunstan Cromarty,

Esquire. *Could not* be interested in him.

He closed his eyes, and rather than stand over him, Jane took a seat on the carpeted floor, which created a curious, eye-level intimacy.

"I'll go home, eventually," he said. "My mother claims she lives for the day, though she's little ones aplenty and all three of my siblings to console her. I'm in practice by myself. All the revenue is mine and all the bills too. You know what that's like."

He had done a better job than Jane had at creating a home. His piano had pictures of *people* on it; family, judging from the number of big, smiling men in kilts. The mantel over the woodstove held framed awards and more pictures, one of them a panoramic photograph of some gray stone castle by a beautiful, still lake.

"Take these," Jane said, passing him two pills. "I found them upstairs. I'm guessing you bought them in the UK, because they have codeine in them and they're not prescription."

"That I did." He downed the pills. "I forgot I had them in my luggage, which doesn't say much for the constabulary in Customs."

A sip of water came next, a tricky undertaking when supine. Jane resisted the urge to support Dunstan's head and took the glass back when he'd finished.

"I've been in Damson County for five years," she said, stroking a hand over Wallace's thick fur, "and I still have boxes of stuff I moved up here from DC. I've thought about switching apartments after the first of the year, but then I'd be committing the mortal sin of moving the same boxes twice."

Dunstan turned his head to offer her a small, conspiratorial smile.

"My boxes are in the garage. I should be in practice with a partner, of course. When I set up shop, I was the new fellow, and I talked funny. Still do, but a partner reduces the risks. You have a partner."

"Not any more. Louise chucked all the glamour and glory of small town legal practice for art school and a certain art professor. Now I have an office big enough for two lawyers and nobody to gripe about it to."

"Gripe to me. I'm a captive audience, and I'm developing an unnatural relationship with the couch and the heating pad both. Wallace has set me a bad example, you see. You, fortunately, are putting my cat to sleep, or he'd be tormenting me in my helpless and vulnerable state."

For all his grousing about the cat, Dunstan was less uncomfortable. Jane deduced this from his eyes, from his color, from the way he relaxed into the sofa cushions. And Wallace wasn't going to sleep. He wouldn't when he was on duty as a guardian kitty of Clan Cromarty's Maryland branch.

"I miss Louise." Jane scratched Wallace's white bib of a chin rather than admit she hadn't meant to say that. "She would come slamming back from court, ranting about Judge Mansfield's bias against people named Horatio, or the prosecutor's inability to organize a docket, and I could come back with lazy opposing counsel and cheating spouses."

"I hate it when they cheat, though I don't blame them. Loneliness is the most dangerous and sincere precursor to stupidity."

He stuffed a pillow under his head, making the muscles of his chest flex, and Jane endured a bolt of sincerity passing right down her middle.

"I can't blame the ones who cheat," Jane said, "but if you'll cheat on your spouse, you'll cheat on your cheat. What sort of foundation is that to move forward on?"

They fell silent while Wallace set up a stentorian purring, co-counsel in agreement with any discussion that kept people close enough to pet him. The cat's expression was knowing and smug, even for a very large, well loved cat.

Insight popped into Jane's mind like Gopher popping up in the middle of the night to visit One Stuck Bear.

Doreen Almquist was cheating.

All of that polish and shine, the time at the gym, the designer wardrobe, the perfect hair, wasn't for the husband she never saw. It was to impress the personal trainer, the sugar daddy—

The guy who bought her all of that jewelry and the fancy perfume.

"You look angry, wee Jane. Is it time for you to leave? Wallace might appreciate a bit of tucker in his dish before you go."

He wouldn't ask for himself, but he'd ask for a cat large enough to have its own gravitational field.

"Family law can be such a trial."

"Put that on a T-shirt, why don't you? Every family law practitioner on the planet would buy it in three different colors."

"I'm abandoning you," Jane said, rising. "Wallace, keep an eye on the patient. I'll be in the kitchen addressing the sore lack of decent victuals on these premises. Dunstan, do you need anything? Once I start cooking, I'm hard to interrupt."

"My files."

"Hopeless," Jane said, though if he could focus on work, then his back was doing better.

Which meant cooking was simply an excuse to stay here, in the half-empty home of a guy Jane could ethically share a professional friendship with—but no more.

***

Wallace at least waited until Jane had disappeared into the kitchen to march across Dunstan's chest and settle on his belly.

"She likes you," Dunstan said. Then more quietly, "I like her."

He reached—carefully—for the Almquist file, then set it aside in favor of the Baxter guardianship, a more or less uncontested matter. Wallace had positioned himself so Dunstan could hold a file too close to read easily or too far away.

"Damned cat."

The Baxter order was well drafted—Trenton Knightley knew what he was about—and the Ostergard pleadings were ready to submit.

Outside, the wind had picked up, and if Dunstan hadn't been nursing his back, he would have loaded up the woodstove. Instead, he pulled the tartan blanket off the back of the couch, suffering Wallace's back claws to his belly for his trouble, only to have the cat re-establish residency when Dunstan had twitched and tugged the blanket into place.

The painkillers were taking effect, subduing the ache in Dunstan's back, while an ache of a different sort rose up in its place.

He subdued that ache with his notes from the Almquists' meeting.

"Something tasty this way comes," Dunstan informed the cat some time later. "Though I don't know what Jane found to cook up. If you were any sort of friend, you'd go on reconnaissance instead of using me for your personal chafing dish."

Jane emerged from the kitchen, a wooden spoon in her hand. "Are you on the phone?"

"Arguing with my cat," Dunstan said, feeling foolish. She'd called his pantry elderly, and old people also talked to their cats. "And winning."

"Ha. Try this." She knelt and held the spoon up to Dunstan's mouth. He took a nibble of tomato, oregano, a hint of cilantro, heat, cumin…

"Does it need something? I like a little heat, a little spice, a hint of sweetness…bold, but not pushy." She tasted from the same spoon Dunstan had, and innuendo blended with the spices, at least in Dunstan's male mind. An image of Jane wearing nothing but her spike heels and a smile—heat, spice, sweetness, and boldness—assaulted him.

"Go for bold," Dunstan said. "The sauce has to stand up to the meat."

"Right. Bold is good. Do you need your glasses?"

He needed a cold shower, which might do permanent damage to his back.

"Aye. Yonder paperweight means I can't view anything from a proper distance." In more ways than one.

"You, come with me." Jane scooped the cat from Dunstan's lap, her hand brushing low across his belly through the blankets. "Leave your buddy in peace so he can deal with his lawyer guilt."

Wallace turned his best take-me-to-your-tuna-fish stare on Jane, while Dunstan put the Ostergard file on his lap. "He's not allowed on the counter."

"Oh, right. All day when you're gone, he sits around staring heavenward, reciting the commandment about not hopping up on spotless counters. He has you so trained."

They disappeared into the kitchen, Jane muttering about stubborn males, Wallace doing his impersonation of a besotted rag doll.

While Dunstan stared at a file that, even with his glasses on, in his present condition, he had little chance of reading.

CHAPTER FOUR

"You must be feeling better," Jane said, though *better* was a relative term. Dunstan had moved from the couch far enough to heed nature's call, and he'd downed a gratifying quantity of chili, but he'd eaten his supper on the couch, a blanket around his shoulders, heating pad at the ready, rather than sitting on a hard kitchen chair.

"I'll manage from here," Dunstan said, jamming a pillow behind his back. "Now it's mostly waiting for the ache to recede while I move about like an old man with a bad hangover."

"You won't overdo?"

"Oh, likely I will, but I've more of those magic pills and your magic chili. You're welcome to take the cat as a sign of my gratitude."

Wallace now sat tucked against Dunstan's side, feline Laird of the Western Couch.

"You can make it up the stairs?"

"That might be a challenge."

Something nagged at Jane, something besides the wish that she could, like a girlfriend, for example, spend the night fussing over him.

In the big bed with the cozy flannel sheets.

"Your house is cold, Dunstan. The kitchen was toasty

because I cooked there, but here and up in the bedroom, you need some heat."

Which observation came out all wrong, factual though it was.

"I haven't serviced the furnace yet this year. The woodstove is normally all I need." He shifted and pushed and came to his feet, looking quite...quite tall wearing nothing but a kilt.

And not at all cold.

"Run along now, Jane. I'll survive."

Run along? Were he not ailing, she would have smacked him for that.

"Show me how to fire this thing up," Jane said, crossing to the squat, black iron stove in the fireplace. "It can't be that difficult."

"It's easy, if you've split enough of the wood that's been seasoning in the garage, which neither I nor Wallace have got 'round to yet."

Dunstan was trying to get rid of her, and that was smart. Then too, wearing only his kilt, he didn't seem affected by the chill seeping into Jane's bones.

"I'm supposed to leave you here, barely able to stand, your house freezing, with no one but that cat to look after you?"

"My back is much better, and by morning I'll be right enough. My bed is cozy, and the roads will only get messier the longer you tarry. Wet leaves can be slicker than ice, even if you have four-wheel drive. Away with you."

Pathetic, that he'd have to shoo her off so determinedly, and yet, Jane could see that even standing upright was costing him.

"The chili's in the fridge," Jane said, taking her coat from the chair she'd tossed it over hours ago. "I fed Wallace some of the Italian sausage when I was cooking, and the corn bread is in the pantry near the whiskey. We never did share that wee dram."

Not that she was about to drink it now, when dark, wet

country roads awaited her.

And a cold apartment without so much as a healthy ficus plant to welcome her.

"My thanks, then," Dunstan said, walking with her to the door. "You're a good cook, Jane DeLuca, but don't worry. Your secret is safe with me."

"And you love your cat," she said, because it was as close to banter as she could dredge up. She found his keys in her coat pocket, shouldered her bag, and prepared to offer him a cheery farewell.

While to herself, she could admit she *liked* this guy. More than liked him, she respected him. How long had it been since a man, any man, had caught her eye? And worse, Dunstan Cromarty, with his cranky devotion to his cat, his Gaelic cussing, and his lonely frugality, caught her by the heart too, and that was—

That was rottenly unfair.

"My thanks," he said again, and while Jane had been silently railing at the universe, Dunstan had moved closer. He still smelled good, of his usual fragrance and some minty muscle rub he'd sneaked onto himself while Jane had done the dishes.

And now, shake hands? Thumbs up with a parting wink? Jaunty salute?

Jane was in her flats, so she had to brace a hand on Dunstan's chest to lean up and kiss his cheek. He held still for it, for the entire, lingering, humiliating, delightful duration of a presuming but not-quite-out-of-bounds parting kiss between friendly associates, and then his arms settled around her.

"If not for you, I'd be stretched out on the floor of my office praying for a coma by now," he muttered. "You're a managing female, and I'm grateful for it. Wallace says the same, and he doesn't give compliments lightly."

Jane's cheek rested against a bare, warm chest, a small fortification against a long, cold, lonely drive home. Jane was further consoled by the notion that nothing she had done with Dunstan, nothing *they* had done, would make facing each other across the conference table or the courtroom any more difficult.

Wonderfully professional of her, all this good behavior.

"I should be going." Dunstan should be letting her go, too.

His cheek came to rest against her hair. "Jane?"

"Hmm?" *Do not kiss this man. Do not lick this man. If you must breathe this man in, do so quietly.*

"The Almquist case calls for full discovery. Proper motions with the court, deadlines, interrogatories, depositions, the whole bit."

Was he *warning* her that his client had colored outside the lines? If so, what warning did she owe him? He wouldn't drop a dime on his own client, which meant he was warning Jane that it really was time for her to leave.

Which it was. Jane stepped back and didn't bother attempting any cheery bullshit, the loss of Dunstan's embrace being about the least cheery misery to befall her since she'd seen a two-time domestic assaulter walk off with custody of his three small children in her first year of practice.

"Full discovery makes sense," she said, though it would drag the case out for months, and the last thing she wanted to deal with any longer than necessary was this *situation* with Dunstan. "Sleep well."

She didn't offer to fetch him anything he might need from the office tomorrow. Let the ever gallant and resourceful Knightley pests perform that chore. Jane had an exceptionally thorough discovery order to draft, nosy interrogatories to pull together, hellacious depositions to plan—

"G'night, then, Jane. Drive carefully and use the seat heater."

He kissed her cheek and winked at her, the barbarian.

Jane opened the door, a blast of frigid, chilly air smacking her in the face. The day had been autumnal. The night—as predicted—had turned wintry.

Behind her, Dunstan began that soft, semi-Gaelic swearing she'd heard from him earlier in the day.

"That's ice coming down out there," he said, tugging Jane back from the door. "It's damned pouring ice, and you're not going anywhere."

***

Western Maryland enjoyed what Uncle Donald would have called Fickle Bitch weather. A November day could be seventeen degrees or seventy degrees, same with February. Whatever plans Dunstan made—to split wood over the coming weekend, for example—the weather could be relied upon to thwart them. After two weeks of Saint Martin's summer—Indian summer, *in American*—winter had apparently descended.

"Sometimes it only starts out with ice then changes back to rain," Jane said, clutching her carpetbag to her chest. "If they've salted the roads, it's probably still safe to drive."

Retreat on her part was smart, because circumstances had conspired to inflict on Dunstan an appreciation for opposing counsel that had only partly to do with her nimble legal mind.

"We'll give it an hour, then, but let's turn on the telly and see what the weather boys and girls have to say. If this is the first storm of the season, they'll be all over it."

"Should we turn on the heat first?"

"Aye, we should, but some frugal Scot hasn't had oil delivered yet this season, and I ran my furnace nigh dry last spring."

March, to be exact, because wood was cleaner and cheaper than oil, and Dunstan enjoyed slamming an ax down on a length of cured oak more than he enjoyed paying the oil bill. A lot more.

She set her bag down, but did not take off her coat. By the time they'd found a weather report, Dunstan was sharing a blanket with Jane on the sofa, Wallace wedged between them like a feline bundling board.

"Ice storms are so pretty," Jane said more than an hour later, "but I hate them. You can't go anywhere, you can't shovel it off, you can't do anything but wait for it to melt and hope the power stays on."

Though for the duration of some movie Dunstan couldn't follow about a hooker falling in love with a young, well-dressed version of Richard Gere, you could cuddle on the couch with a woman who tempted you to highly unprofessional behavior.

You could take more pain medication. You could eat a second helping of very good chili.

"I've only the one bed, Jane, but it has a mattress warmer. You'll be cozy up there."

Or you could argue with a woman half your size and twice your fight about where to sleep.

"You need a decent night's sleep, Dunstan. I can curl up here with Wallace."

He reasoned, he taunted, he considered getting her drunk, but in his present condition. he couldn't carry her up the steps anyway, so he did what few Scots had ever learned to do well, he retreated.

She was gracious, agreeing to keep the heating pad with her. She pulled a pink plastic bag from her Mary Poppins satchel and disappeared into the bathroom.

Being only a fool rather than a very great fool, Dunstan used her absence to totter up the stairs, though he could feel Wallace's smirk with each careful, uneven step.

Wallace was likely overcome by hilarity when, around one in the morning, Dunstan woke to realize the power was out. His bed was delightfully cozy, but the battery backup on his digital alarm clock was blinking madly, the mattress warmer had cut off, and the house was swaddled in a profound silence that suggested not even the fridge was running.

Jane would manage—she had Wallace, she had a wool blanket. She'd curled up in her coat, too.

By one thirty a.m., when Dunstan got up to use the

facilities, those arguments weren't keeping him warm, much less the lady he found shifting restlessly on his couch.

"Come up to bed, Jane. You'll catch your death down here."

"You sh-should not have come down those stairs in the dark, Dunstan Cromarty. The EMTs are likely overwhelmed with calls tonight, and I'll be fine as long as Wallace—"

The cat hopped off the couch and strutted, tail up, for the kitchen.

"Come to bed," Dunstan said, extending a hand down to her. "I canna sleep thinking you're shivering away in my own house, while I'm warm and toasty between my flannel sheets."

She pushed the blanket aside and rose, though Dunstan did not flatter himself she cared for his tender sensibilities. The lady was enamored of his Black Watch plaid flannel sheets, lest there be any mistaking the matter.

He used his cell phone as a flashlight as he herded Jane up the stairs, then switched it off, because a bad storm could kill the power for days.

Jane draped her coat over his reading chair and dove under the covers.

"Cromarty, you are an honest man. This bed is h-heaven."

Heaven for her, hell for him. "Move over. You're on my side."

"Use the other side. I'm calling dibs on this one until spring thaw."

Arguing was what lawyers did. It was also what lovers did. Dunstan climbed in on the far side, the cool bedding providing no distraction whatsoever from his bedmate.

She shivered, which made the bed tremble, and created a dilemma for Dunstan having moral, ethical, pragmatic, erotic, and even—he *was* an honest man—romantic implications.

Which he would consider when the electricity came back on, or while waiting tables at some dive in Edinburgh, the sure fate of those disbarred for gross misconduct.

"Come here, wee Jane. You'll keep me awake with your

shivering, and I need my beauty sleep."

He also needed his license to practice law, though it would not keep him warm under these covers. Neither would Jane's license perform that function for her.

"You come here," she said. "The feeling has come back in my feet, and I'm not budging."

He rolled to his side, tucked her against his chest, and wondered how many other former members of the bar had mentally practiced the question, *May I supersize that for you?*

***

Dunstan was warm, he smelled good, and he was warm. Any two of the three would have sufficed to send Jane's scruples out into the icy, blustery night. She scooted around to face him, bundled into his chest, and hiked her legs over his hips. Dunstan brought his thighs up under her backside and wrapped an arm around her middle, and everywhere, he was *warm*.

"Try to relax," he said. "Relax in your middle. You'll stop shivering sooner."

"Where's Wallace when you need him?"

"The bedroom door's open, and heat rises, so this is probably the least cold room in the house. He'll be upon us soon, literally."

A madness was upon Jane, a madness to exercise awful judgment with Dunstan Cromarty at least three times before morning. She wouldn't jeopardize her license to practice for anything less than a hat trick.

"Dunstan?"

"Go to sleep, Jane."

As if. "Even Wallace ignores you when you give orders like that. You're becoming aroused." With reassuring speed, too.

"I'm also over the age of thirty, and thus not at the mercy of my biology." He sounded amused, while he felt…

"I wouldn't mind being at the mercy of your biology."

A considering sort of silence ensued, while Jane's teeth

stopped chattering and Dunstan's embrace became less utilitarian.

"You'd mind if we crossed that line, Jane. When we're in court, the Almquists snarling at each other, the accusations flying, the judge fed up with the lot of us, you'd mind that I knew exactly how your breasts felt in my hands. You wouldn't want me knowing the taste of you, and you'd hate that you knew the taste of me, or the feel of me as I—go to sleep."

Until that moment, Jane might have been content with a rousing argument, a lecture about professional integrity and circumstances conspiring, but Dunstan's burr rumbling through the darkness, his scent, his heat, put images in her head of intimacy and pleasure.

"I'll get out of the case," she said, kissing his chest. Of course, she'd get out of the case—easiest thing in the world to file a motion to strike her appearance and enter somebody else's.

Anybody else's.

Dunstan's hand landed in her hair, cradling her closer. "You need the money. So do I."

"No, we don't need it. We just want it. People get divorced every thirty seconds in this country. I haven't wanted to be intimate with a man for—"

He kissed her cheek. "Hush, woman. Please, God, hush."

"—years, and you're in worse shape than I am," Jane went on, this time kissing his throat. "You hush, and—"

His hand, big and warm, palmed her breast through her old T-shirt. "I'll get out of the case, too, if you'll only for the love of Almighty—"

She got her mouth on his, and while his body was warm, his mouth was *hot*. Blessedly, desperately hot.

Dunstan tried to draw back for about two seconds, but then Jane felt the instant when his professionalism lost the case entirely to the logic of loneliness and desire. He shifted so she was half-tucked under him, and his weight was the most delightful reassurance that Jane would stay warm through the night.

His tongue was a wonder on cross-examination, feinting, teasing, daring—

"Clothes," Jane managed. He drew back enough that she could get out of her sweats and T-shirt without gelding him or giving him a black eye, though it was a near thing on both counts.

"Take off my kilt," he said.

"You take it—" What the hell, *of course* she'd take his kilt off. She found the buckles and wrenched them loose. Then she found *him*.

"Careful," he whispered, "or this exercise in confused priorities will be over before it starts."

"Will not," Jane said, stroking her fingers down the hard, silky length of him. But having made the decision to be intimate with Dunstan, her sense of urgency abated, leaving her curiously bereft.

How long had it been since she'd reciprocated a man's desire for her? Since she'd felt that lovely contrast, between the soft underside of her breast and the callused tenderness of a male palm?

Was this what family law had done to her? Made her avoid the very relationships that could give life meaning?

"Where did you go, Jane?" Dunstan asked, his hand shaping breast.

"I'm here," she said, cradling his check against her palm. "Why did we become lawyers, Dunstan?"

He should have laughed at the question, for it was no kind of pillow talk. Instead, he offered the first year law student's answer. "To do good while doing well?"

She thought of Doreen Almquist's perfect hair and her bewildered ex-to-be holding her as she cried in a cold, wet parking lot.

"Are we doing either?"

"On a good day, I hope. I'll tell you a secret," he said, nuzzling her neck. "I'm no damned good at math, and I like to argue. That's why I'm a lawyer."

"That was why you went to law school, but it's not why you're a good lawyer."

From the jumbled heap of arousal, self-doubt, and career puzzlement, Jane extracted a truth:

She liked, respected, and was attracted to Dunstan Cromarty, and with good reason. He was a singularly worthy man. Giving up a case that wasn't likely to go well was no price to pay for exploring where that attraction might lead.

Getting into bed with him was the smartest move she'd made in years.

"You don't want to be in bed with the lawyer, good or otherwise," Dunstan said, tracing his finger over her lips. "And neither do I, so could we please dispense with the questioning?"

She bit his finger, gently, because he'd said *please.* "I want this to matter, Dunstan, and I want to savor it. I want it hot and slow, and—"

"And I want *you.*" He eased his finger over her lips. "*Now.* Reach into the top drawer and find us a Frenchie."

"I'm on the pill, and I don't even know what a Frenchie—"

He cut off whatever closing arguments she might have appended with a slow, deep, wet kiss that made Jane's insides sing something other than *Auld Lang Syne.* She kissed him back, climbed over him, and prepared to argue with him about who would be on top of whom.

The first time.

"Dunstan, are you comfortable on your back?"

"Aye, except for a wee ache in m' goolies."

"What are—?"

He nudged up. *Those* goolies.

"I ache too, and I don't even have goolies," she said, scraping her nails over his nipples.

"We'll let that be our secret. For much of the male bar

association would have it otherwise when they oppose you."

He trapped her hands, and the moment became serious. The air Jane breathed was cold, probably cold enough that she could see her breath, but the entire house was in darkness. The clicky-wet sound of ice hitting the windows underscored the sense that beneath the covers, with Dunstan, was the only heat Jane would find anywhere.

"Love me," she whispered, right against his lips.

Dunstan Cromarty went about his loving the way he prosecuted his cases—thoroughly, with attention to detail, nothing sloppy or haphazard. When Jane might have rushed through their initial coupling, he slowed her down, with naughty whispers, soft caresses, and a patient, almost stealthy joining of their bodies.

"You feel,"—Jane cast around for a word to capture the way he filled her up, inexorably, sweetly, powerfully, completely—"*sublime*. If you don't let me catch my breath, I'll come, Dunstan."

He didn't let her catch her breath. Not the first time, or the second. By the third, though, Jane had found that Dunstan Cromarty had sensitive earlobes—something nobody had bothered to discover with him previously—and she could drive him to distraction with just her mouth.

"You have much to answer for," Dunstan whispered. "Taking advantage of my delicate back, driving me 'round the bend with your naughty mouth. The time has come for you to pay, Jane DeLuca."

He was strong, and determined, and because Jane was on top, Dunstan's hands were free to torment her, and torment her, he did. He worked his thumb between them and applied a steady pressure to a part of Jane already gone screamingly sensitive.

And if this was Dunstan with a delicate back…

"Damn you," Jane panted when pleasure blossomed, hot and relentlesse, once again. "You too, Dunstan."

With her last shred of strategy, she took his earlobe between her finger and thumb and pinched hard and that, ah yes, *that*.

"Yes. Yes, *yes*, Dunstan Lachlan Cromarty—"

He covered her mouth with his, while bliss shimmered through Jane, brighter, longer, more than she could endure, and yet, endure it she did, for Dunstan endured it with her.

She would have pitched off him immediately, the better to breathe and reactivate her brain, but Dunstan's embrace prevented it.

"Give me a minute," he said. "Please. Tissues are on the night table."

She would give him years, if he were inclined to take them. "Your back's okay?"

"Bugger my back. My earlobes will glow for a week."

He sounded pleased, and his hand drifting over Jane's back was so tender that tears threatened. She snuggled closer. "If I had goolies, they'd glow for a month."

He kissed her temple, and Jane remained snuggled to his chest, fighting sleep and tears both, because she did have a heart, and as delicate as extricating herself from the Almquist case would be, trying to disentangle herself from the man sharing the bed with her would be impossible.

***

"He won't let me out."

Jane sounded panicked, though her panic was controlled.

Dunstan closed the Ostergard file and switched the phone to his left ear, because the right one was still a tad sore about the earlobe.

"Whether an attorney leaves a case isn't up to the client, Jane. You send him the explanatory letter, and you file the motion."

"I know that," she spat, for of course, he should not have presumed to lecture her on legal procedure. "I told him I had a potential conflict of interest I hadn't known about when

I took the case, and I'm ethically required to get out of the case."

Not a potential conflict of interest, a real conflict. Dunstan hardly blamed her for putting it more delicately to her client. He would put it the same way to Doreen.

"And?"

"He said he'd waive the conflict. Seems accountants deal with conflict of interest occasionally too."

"Bloody hell. I haven't been able to reach Doreen. Let me think."

"How's your back?"

His back? He'd found the sure cure for his back, though the interlude with Jane played hell with his conscience.

"My back is fine, thank you. Chili for breakfast is my new favorite medicinal."

A silence fell, awkward, wishful. They spoke at the same time.

"I've been meaning to make something clear—" From Jane.

"Would you ever consider—?" From Dunstan.

He did not want to endure whatever she'd been meaning to make clear, because women who wanted more from a man they'd spent the night with—the night loving him to exhaustion—didn't sneak off in the morning, then wait three days to call the fellow.

"If you have to be specific with Calvin," Dunstan said, "then be specific. We were both in that bed, Jane, and we're both adults. I'll be getting out of the case too, as soon as I can get Doreen to return my calls."

"Divorce clients are like that," she said. "They bombard you with calls over nothing, then go to ground when you need an urgent signature."

She'd probably complained about that to the absent Louise, while Dunstan griped to his cat about the same thing.

"This isn't urgent," Dunstan said. "Nobody has filed

anything."

Back to the legalities, when he wanted to ask her if she was wearing shoes, and if so, were they the spiky kind or the little black slippers.

"When are you supposed to meet with Calvin again?" he asked, though why wouldn't a guy with his hand in the till, or hiding marital assets, be eager to delay the divorce proceedings any way he could?

"He said he'd get back to me, but that I'm staying in the case."

"Did he tell you why?" Though Dunstan knew why: Jane was damned good.

If she were subjected to disciplinary action because of something Dunstan could have prevented, he would not forgive himself.

"He said I'm not in it for the money."

"Smart man. You're not, but why did he say that?" Dunstan considered switching the phone again—his left earlobe had some residual soreness too—but he liked the reminder of what Jane DeLuca could do when wearing no shoes.

"I'm forever badgering him to get into counseling. For himself, for Doreen, for the kids. The family's entire upkeep lands on Calvin's shoulders, and I don't want my guy to fall apart."

And her client sensed that, sensed her concern.

"I've told Doreen the same thing. She doesn't think Calvin will spend the money."

The silence was more thoughtful, more lawyerly, and sadder.

"That loneliness stuff again," Jane said. "Making fools of us."

"Jane, promise me you won't do anything rash or heroic. It wasn't loneliness—" His second line beeped. "Hold on. This might be Doreen."

"I'll wait."

Dunstan hit the rollover line button, half-hoping it was Doreen.

"We still on for lunch?" MacKenzie Knightley, the guy everybody took to lunch when they had a tough criminal case to deal with.

"Hello, Mac. I'd forgotten we'd scheduled lunch today." Forgotten pretty much everything having to do with running a law office.

"Now or never," Mac said. "I have an attempted murder coming up for trial, and my dance card is getting full. We can reschedule, but don't expect me to desecrate poker night with shop talk."

The light on Dunstan's first line winked out.

Bloody hell.

"Of course not. Poker night is so I can listen to three grown men fret over what to get one small girl for Christmas." For Trenton Knightley's daughter had no more devoted uncles than Mac and James.

"So listen to me fret over lunch too," Mac said. "I'm in the mood for something besides a chicken salad or a tuna melt."

"Mexican," Dunstan said, because the only person he'd eat Eritrean with—the person he'd gladly surrender his license to practice law for—had just hung up on him.

CHAPTER FIVE

"*Louise?*" Jane was so surprised to see her former partner she'd inadvertently pushed the wrong button and cut Dunstan off instead of putting him on hold. "Damn, your timing stinks. Take a load off and gimme a minute to finish this call."

She started to redial, then realized Louise would overhear every word, and Louise was still a member of the bar. As in, Louise could be questioned in connection with any grievance brought against another member of the bar.

Thinking like a lawyer sometimes sucked rotten eggs.

"Tough case?" Louise asked as Jane put the receiver back on its cradle.

"Yes—no. Yes and no. How have you been?"

"Art school is wonderful."

The school was up in York, Pennsylvania, better than an hour's drive on a chilly, sloppy day, and Louise was not giving off the wonderful vibe.

"And?"

"And I'm thinking of quitting the job."

Jane came around the desk to take the second guest chair. "Lou, you saved for years to make this jump. You put up with Judge Mansfield, did DUIs until your eyes crossed, and you're thinking of throwing in the towel? Does this have to do with a man?"

Louise examined her nails, which were naked—not lacquered, polished, or even manicured. Clay was her favorite medium, and hard on the hands.

"Maybe with the absence of a man. Robert informed me last week he's considering a design job in New York."

New York was the brass ring in the design field, the Holy Grail, the Supreme Court of the United States—according to the designers working in New York.

"Bastard."

"Oh, maybe, but I shouldn't have changed careers to chase a guy."

"I didn't think you were."

Louise was a beautiful woman. Tall, with dark auburn hair, chocolate-brown eyes, and a killer figure, she should have been an artist's model, if nothing else.

And she was sad, which on her had the gall to look even prettier.

"I didn't think I was chasing a guy, either," she said. "But now Robert's off for the bright lights, and I'm left in good old P-A, trying not to wince every time somebody says 'you-inz' and wondering what was so awful about the practice of law."

Robert was an okay guy, but he didn't look at Louise the way Louise looked at fresh clay and an afternoon free to spend with her wheel.

"You're thinking of transferring to a school in New York?"

Louise rose and went to the dish garden, testing the dampness of the moss with her finger, then using Eeyore to give the moss a drink.

"That hadn't even occurred to me. Do you have court this afternoon?"

"No." Thank God. Because at the courthouse, she might run into Dunstan, and that would be lovely and awful and difficult and wonderful. Until she was out of the Almquist case, a dram of avoidance would be worth a cask of disbarment.

"If you don't have court, then let's go to lunch," Louise said, shrugging back into her coat.

"Lou, I was in the middle of a phone call. An important phone call."

"Whoever it was didn't call you back, did they?" She tossed Jane her coat and shouldered Jane's carpetbag. "Call them after lunch, because I need somebody to talk sense into me, and you're all I've got."

"We'll discuss a hypothetical or two, because I need some sense talked into me too."

"No, you don't. You aren't the risk-taking kind, and that's why you didn't waste thousands of dollars relocating for an adjunct position so you could teach drawing to a bunch of fashionably emaciated waifs ten years your junior."

"We used to be waifs, Lou. Where are we going?" Jane had to hustle, because Louise on a mission was a long-legged, fast-moving train.

"Someplace spicy. Cold weather works up my appetite, and I haven't found any decent restaurants yet near school. Why didn't I think of offering to go to New York with Robert?"

"I dunno. If a certain Scotsman told me he was heading home, I would at least hint about a willingness to visit him there."

Louise slowed to Mach One. "A *Scotsman*?"

Jane grabbed her by the elbow when she would have stepped off the curb. "Mexican's the closest. Tell me about these guys ten years younger than you."

The distraction worked, at least temporarily, but Jane hadn't been entirely honest with her friend.

If Dunstan went back to Scotland to stay, Jane would offer to go with him, and hang the immigration laws.

Hang all the damned laws.

***

"So how're things?" Mac asked. "Has Judge Blaisdale quoted any Shakespeare at you lately?"

When Blaisdale got out the Shakespeare, somebody's client was going down hard in the yard, as the denizens of the Detention Center put it.

"Not for a couple weeks," Dunstan replied. "You're having a taco salad? How is that different from a chicken salad?" And which case was it that had prompted Dunstan to schedule lunch with MacKenzie Knightley?

"I'm having a taco salad with rice and beans. Carbohydrates fuel the brain," Mac said, catching the waitress's eye.

Carby bliss fueled the brain.

"May we have some lemon for our water?" Mac asked. Nothing about MacKenzie Knightley was flirtatious—not one damned thing—but the waitress beamed at him as if his every wish was her darkest fantasy come true.

"How do you do that?" Dunstan asked, tucking his tie away. "How do you appeal to the ladies without so much as batting your eyes?"

Mac took a sip of Dos Equis—no heather ale here. "Maybe the ladies can sense I'm no threat. I'm not buying, they don't have to sell, and we can all relax."

Dunstan could not relax. Why had Jane hung up on him?

"Attempted murder keeps you warm at night?"

"The woodstove keeps me warm at night, Cromarty, and most other times. You have lady trouble."

Dunstan left off staring at the beer menu—whose idea had it been to do Mexican?—while Mac watched him patiently.

"How ever can you tell such a thing, MacKenzie?"

Mac waited until the smiling waitress dropped off a dish of lemon wedges arranged in an artful pinwheel.

"I have two little brothers, one of whom has been through such a nasty divorce, he's practically a monk. The other is the equivalent of a temple whore, stepping out with any dumped, divorced, or desperate woman. I know when the ladies are giving a guy fits, Cromarty. Sooner or later, everybody gets a turn in that barrel."

Which left the question of when Mac had taken his turn, or was he still taking it?

"So let's consider a hypothetical," Dunstan said. "Family law case, two competent attorneys, parties still talking but not exactly cordial. The money isn't adding up, somebody has income they're not disclosing, probably opposing counsel's client, and opposing counsel may or may not know what's afoot. The lawyers have a wee, private lapse and get a bit too affectionate on one occasion—"

"You get out of the case," Mac said. "You both get your sorry, besotted, unethical asses out of the case, and you never, ever oppose each other—unless you're James Knightley."

"*What?*"

Mac squeezed three lemon wedges over his water glass. Something about the dispatch with which he pulverized his citrus reminded Dunstan that the guy also shoed horses.

"Trent and I have our suspicions about our baby brother, and it's all but bar association fact the state's attorney was tying 'em on with Danica Showalter before she went to rehab."

Danica was—had been—a criminal defense attorney. Nobody seemed to know what had become of her after her second trip through rehab.

"Am I supposed to derive comfort from the notion that our very own bar association is less than angelic?"

"Yes," Mac said, passing the remaining lemons over to Dunstan. "You're also supposed to get out of the case."

The pretty pinwheel wasn't half so appealing with three mangled wedges among its number.

"The clients in this purely hypothetical example aren't cooperating. One has said he'll waive any conflict, though the exact nature of the problem hasn't yet been explained to him. I suspect the second will follow suit."

Mac again waited until the food had been set on the table, such was his inherent discretion.

"Eat your food, Cromarty. Though why anybody would

go to a Mexican restaurant and tell them to hold the rice and beans, I do not know. Who has your knickers in an uproar?"

Not his knickers, his earlobes, his law practice, everything between his earlobes, and his—

The cheery little bell over the door jingled, and who should walk in, but Jane DeLuca and her former law partner. Dunstan wanted to wave, wanted to tackle the woman where she stood—in furry brown boots with low heels—but instead, he took a bite of whatever he'd ordered.

"We were discussing a hypothetical, Mac." For Jane either hadn't seen him, or was ignoring him altogether.

"Cromarty, stop looking pathetic. You're a grown man, and if Jane DeLuca has given you the time of day, so to speak, you're the first to breach that citadel in living memory."

"I would also like to be the last." If nothing else had come clear during the past three days of mooning at his phone like a lovesick juvenile, that had.

"Your clients are in the middle of a divorce when they themselves are likely tempted by all sorts of stupid impulses. Yes, the bar association will take a dim view of what has happened, but you'll probably get away with a suspension—a pair of suspensions."

Across the busy restaurant, Jane slid into a booth opposite Louise. Coats were shuffled aside, the Mary Poppins rucksack stayed by Jane's side, and beneath the table, her boots remained on her feet.

"Jane DeLuca will not be suspended. I'll turn in my license before I'll allow that to happen."

"Then the condemned should enjoy a last meal. What did you order anyway?"

"Food." Dunstan put a twenty on the table. "I hope you and Louise get along, because I'm kidnapping a member of the bar for nefarious purposes."

"Those are the best kind," Mac said, slipping the twenty into his wallet. "Kidnapping is a felony, please recall."

Dunstan left Mac sipping his beer and muttering a line from *MacBeth*: *Confusion now hath made his masterpiece.*

***

"Ladies, hello."

Jane left off fishing for tissues in The Vast Lonely, because that voice was the last one she'd expected to hear.

Her Every Stupid Wish loomed over the table, looking serious, tired, and dear. "Dunstan. A pleasure to see you. You and Louise know each other?"

"Of course we do, though MacKenzie Knightley is in want of a lunch companion, and I was hoping Louise would oblige."

"What are friends for?" Louise said, abandoning the field without giving Jane a chance to tromp on her foot under the table. "Mac is always good company."

She was across the restaurant in half a heartbeat.

"And what am I?" Jane muttered, "chopped livva?"

"You are coming with me," Dunstan said. "You don't leave a man with sore earlobes and then not call him for three days."

Across the restaurant, Louise waved while MacKenzie Knightley saluted with his beer and winked.

"Please, Jane. Will you walk with me?"

"We are still counsel of record," Jane hissed, scooting out of the booth. "You can't tell me about your earlobes, and I can't tell you about my—"

He held her coat for her, just as if they were a couple of longstanding. "Your what?"

With her back to him, she could interrupt her flight of lawyer nerves to ask, "Why didn't you call me?"

His hands stroked over her shoulders, fleetingly. "One doesn't want to presume."

She turned and flipped her hair out of her collar. "Bull-poo-poo, Cromarty."

"Very well," he said, preceding her to the door and holding it for her. "I wanted to get out of the case before I contacted you again. That plan isn't working."

"We are in such doo-doo," Jane said, while Dunstan scooted around her to take the position closer to the street.

"No, we are not," Dunstan retorted, with the air of a man who had spent all night rehearsing his closing argument.

And then somebody's phone chimed to the tune of *Scotland the Brave*.

"Fook."

"At least it's not Dixie," Jane said, while Dunstan held his phone to his ear.

He went still, dark brows drawing down. "Yes, Doreen. I'll contact Ms. DeLuca. Two o'clock?"

He shot Jane a questioning glance, and she nodded, for this afternoon she had neither clients nor court appearances nor common sense.

"My office, then, and yes, I'll make sure Ms. DeLuca's there too."

He slipped his phone into a pocket, while Jane tried to memorize what was good about the moment, for it might be among their last as practicing attorneys. Dunstan's expression was impassive, blaming nobody, and that was good.

Jane was healthy, had some cash stashed, and no ficus plant depending on her.

That was good too.

"Wallace can survive a long time on half rations," she said. "And I want to take your hand right here on the street. Those are good things, Dunstan. I don't eat much when I'm nervous, and that's probably a good thing too. I have tissues in my purse, and that's a very good thing."

Dunstan was a resourceful guy. He didn't take her hand, there on the street for all to see, but he winged his elbow, like an old-fashioned gentleman might, when the way was slippery, and a lady could fall on her backside at any moment.

***

"Doreen and Calvin would like to meet with us," Dunstan said, though that wasn't quite accurate. Doreen had *demanded* another four-way meeting and had said Calvin would confirm that request with his attorney if necessary.

Calvin, whose position earlier had been to waive any conflicts of interest, was now demanding a four-way meeting.

"Here's another good thing," Jane said. "When I'm in a situation where my law practice can be taken from me, I realize I like being a lawyer. Yes, we have hard days, but what goes on in the courthouse is a big improvement over the ducking stool and the lynch mob. I like being part of solving people's legal problems."

Such comforting images, the ducking stool and the lynch mob.

"This is what we tell our clients, then," Dunstan said. "We tell them I made untoward advances to you, and that's why we're getting out of the case. You can report me to the bar association, and they'll slap my wrist,"—probably with the disciplinary equivalent of a sledgehammer—"and I'll be able to sleep at night."

Maybe even with Jane?

She stopped right in the middle of the sidewalk. "That would be lying, Dunstan. I'm the one who propositioned you."

American English was not a language for the faint of heart.

"You extended an invitation, which I was more than free to decline, Jane. Both of us need not suffer the consequences."

She got the same look in her eye she'd had when Dunstan had told her to run along.

"Dunstan, do you *want* to be sent back to Scotland with your tail between your legs? Do you *want* to spend the next twenty years teaching the same constitutional law cases at the Podunk Highland School of Law and Hangover Remedies?"

He took her arm and resumed their stroll toward the legal gallows.

"Here we come to one of your good things, though why you'd focus on such a litany at this juncture, I do not know. Now, when I'm faced with losing my livelihood, and returning to Scotland is the only reasonable choice, I find instead I want to buy the house I'm living in, get Wallace some company for the long days he's stuck at home, and otherwise anchor myself here more thoroughly."

Jane was part of that, but not all of it. Taking a cat to Europe was no easy feat.

"But Scotland is home," Jane said, ever the advocate—for anybody but herself. "Scotland is where you have nieces and nephews and the wee whatevers, and everybody can understand you when you cuss."

"You can understand me when I don't cuss. You can understand me when I don't say anything at all."

He should not have said that. Jane fell silent, no argument, no motions, no cross-examination as they ambled along.

"We're not lying to our clients, Dunstan. That's not the kind of lawyers we are."

Now was his turn to argue, to point out that if they put the bald truth on the table, they wouldn't be any kind of lawyers at all. They waited on a corner for the light to change, though no traffic moved in either direction.

"You're sure, Jane?"

A leaf drifted by, one of the last golden remnants of the venerable oak.

"I would like to see Scotland someday," she said. "I'd like that a lot. I can't imagine an entire country where everybody sounds like you."

Well, then. He walked along beside his Jane, a lightness suffusing him, despite the afternoon's agenda.

Get fired.

Refund an entire retainer despite hours spent on the case.

Begin long, messy, ultimately costly disciplinary proceedings.

Shut down a law practice after years of trying to build it up.

And finish falling in love.

Not a bad day's work.

He stopped outside the building housing Jane's office, which was around the block from his. "I'll see you at two. Mind you, don't leave me to face the dragons alone."

As if she would.

Jane stretched up to kiss his cheek. "Until two."

***

What sort of man offers to ruin his career for a single night of—

Not sex.

Lovemaking? And cuddling, and talking. And more lovemaking, and sore earlobes, and sore…

Jane took the place across from Dunstan at his lovely conference table and pulled the Almquist file out of her bag, the Complaint for Limited Divorce right on top. Dunstan had on his glasses, his yellow legal pad at the ready, business as usual—except this was every lawyer's worst nightmare.

And he was ready to face it with her.

"This shouldn't take long," Calvin said.

Across the table, Dorie watched him, and not with the guarded, bitchy expression of a woman preparing to do battle. She wore jeans and a UMBC sweatshirt, while Cal was in jeans, a blue button-down, and a tan corduroy jacket.

Counseling, then. They'd finally started counseling. Dunstan must have sensed this too, because under the stable, a large foot gently nudged at Jane's boot.

"We have as much time as you need," Dunstan said. "And we're not on the clock."

Of course they weren't. Jane nudged him back: *Good call.*

"Tell them, Cal," Dorie said. "It's not complicated."

No, it was not, though where was Calvin's triple-steel reinforced Underwriters Laboratory-approved briefcase?

"My attorney said something that got me thinking," Calvin said. "Jane said that I hadn't kept a close enough eye on the household account. I'm the accountant in the family, and I leave all that for Dorie to manage."

"I don't mind," Dorie said. "You put in enough hours with the numbers."

They exchanged a look, a married-couple-shorthand look Jane couldn't quite fathom. Divorces weren't always nasty, though they were usually sad, and that look had held regret, at least.

"In any case," Calvin went on, "I couldn't get that observation out of my mind, and I began to look, really look, at what it takes to keep our house going. Having a new water heater installed on an emergency basis was hundreds of dollars. If we'd picked one up ourselves, and I'd taken a Saturday morning to install it—the boys would have helped, would have learned a few things."

A regret phase then, but where were the Almquists headed with this?

"Cal asked to see the checkbook," Dorie said, spreading her hands out flat on the conference table. Today her nails were plain, and she wore no rings—suggesting they'd found a *good* counselor. "At first I thought Cal was snooping, looking for how I'd wasted his hard-earned money."

"Our hard-earned money," Cal interjected.

"But then I figured, he's still my husband, and we won't get through this divorce by stealing from each other. I showed him the real checkbook."

Dunstan shot Jane a perplexed look, but kept his thoughts and his toes to himself.

"Dorie keeps excellent records," Cal said. "I'm an accountant, and I couldn't see what any fool would have seen."

"I didn't want you to see, Vinnie."

"And I can't see," Jane said. "What did you find in those records, Calvin?"

"I found my wife."

Across the table, husband and wife visually held hands. Dunstan saw it too, because he pushed his yellow legal pad aside, put his pen down, and took off his glasses.

"My lawyer, who has never set foot in my house, picked up on what I'd been blind to," Calvin said. "One income isn't enough to sustain the lifestyle we enjoy. Dorie has been tutoring college kids in English, and what I assumed were trips to the gym, lunches with the ladies, and tennis games were Dorie's way of bringing in extra money without making me feel inadequate."

"It's not that much," Dorie said. "And I like helping young people learn. I have a master's in English, and I wasn't doing anything with it. And I would have told Cal soon, because we file our taxes jointly. A 1099 is a tough thing to hide from a CPA. Besides, Dunstan saw the same thing Jane did and was about to go all lawyer on the household financial records. I'd rather Cal learned the truth from me."

"I lost sight of my marriage, but Dorie is right: I would have noticed a statement of income earned, but I'd become blind to my own wife. What does that say about me and my own accountability?"

"It says you're human," Dunstan suggested. "Does this mean you'll go to counseling?"

Dorie tucked her hair back behind her ear, a curiously girlish gesture. "It means we went to bed—well, the utility closet first. And the shower, and then—"

"Sweetie." Calvin's tone was indulgent—or smug? "I don't think a pair of divorce lawyers needs to know those details."

"No," Jane said. "We don't." *The utility closet?* "So where do you want to go from here with the lawsuit?"

"Nowhere," Dorie replied. "Cal will telecommute two days a week outside of tax season, I'll try to limit my tutoring to the other three days, and we'll get back to being married."

"You might still consider counseling," Dunstan said.

"Maybe." The look in Cal's eyes promised his wife more trips to the utility closet too.

"I'll be getting my checkbook, then," Dunstan said, rising. "And I'll forward to Doreen the contents of the file after I've had a chance to copy them."

When the door had closed, Doreen appropriated Dunstan's legal pad and pen and began to doodle.

"Is there any point telling that man to keep his checkbook?" she asked.

"None, and I have mine with me too," Jane said, though it took a moment of fishing to find it. "I'm happy for you folks. This doesn't happen often, but I'm always glad when it does."

Calvin sidled around the table to take the seat Dunstan had vacated. "I liked that about you, that you pushed me toward reconciliation and counseling."

"I don't always," Jane said, scrawling out a check. "Each case is different. Then too, sometimes the devil you know is the very best devil for you."

She pushed the check across to Calvin, who had to inspect the amount.

"This is for the full retainer," he said. "That's not what we agreed to. I'm happy to pay—"

Doreen put her hand over his mouth. "Say thank you, Calvin."

He kissed her fingers, and Jane nearly had to open a window. "Thank you, Jane, but why?"

Tell the client the truth that matters most. "Because this case has done my heart good."

Doreen left off flirting with her husband long enough to peer at Jane. "Dunstan's not a bad-looking guy, you know, though he's a little on the imposing side. He seems kinda lonely to me, all work and no play. You two might get along. You should think about it."

Jane was preserved from stammering a reply when the not-bad-looking guy himself came back into the room, check in hand.

"Best of luck, folks," he said, handing Dorie her refund.

"Now, see what I mean?" Dorie said. "This is for the full amount too, and you two didn't even have to consult each other about it. You might get along with each other better than you think. Honey, put this in the Christmas fund, would you?"

"I think we should start a second-honeymoon fund," Calvin said, getting to his feet and tucking the check away. "Or maybe an annual honeymoon fund."

"Out," Dunstan said, pointing toward the door. "And never come back, because we willna represent you for any amount of money. Consider Scotland for one of those holidays, though. It's beautiful any time of year."

Doreen took Calvin by the hand, patted Dunstan's cheek, and winked at Jane.

And then they were gone.

Saved by the utility closet.

***

"Is Scotland lovely any time of year?" Jane asked, tossing her checkbook into that great bag of hers.

What was she really asking?

"Depends on what part of Scotland. One area in the northwest gets close to sixteen feet of rainfall a year. A lot of our sadder, drunker ballads are from that region."

"I'm neither sad nor drunk," Jane said, running her fingers over the surface of the conference table. "I'm really, really relieved."

Dunstan took the place beside her, purely for the pleasure of proximity to her, not because his own knees were feeling weak. "We had a near miss."

"I don't like that I put the cart before the horse," Jane said. "I should have kept my pants on, withdrawn from the case, then jumped your bones."

He prayed there was a but coming. "I'm not proud of myself in that regard, either."

"Is there a but coming?"

Dunstan could tell from how Jane scooted a bit that beneath the table, she was shuffling off her boots.

"Yes. Yes, there is a but, or a however. We're good at what

we do, Jane."

"Very good, which excuses nothing."

The temptation to take her hand was nearly befuddling him, but he wanted to put his reasoning before her.

"We both know the rules, and for my part, when you gave me the opportunity, I put a higher value on sharing intimacies with you than I did on my continued ability to practice law."

The grain of the chestnut surface apparently fascinated Jane, because she studied it as if it were an original manuscript of the first Supreme Court opinion handed down.

"Jane?"

"What you're saying is, if you had it to do over again, even knowing we might be disbarred, even knowing it wasn't smart or professional, you would have done the same thing—and so would I. What does that say about us, Dunstan? As attorneys, sworn to uphold the law, as officers of the court?"

The answer to her question had kept him up for two nights, and it did matter—some.

"It says the law is important to us, but we're more important to each other. In this one instance, I can live with that revelation. I can even rejoice in it. I've never misstepped like this before, Jane, and I certainly don't intend to again."

He trapped her hand in his, lest she stroke the finish right off the conference table.

She turned her hand palm up and laced her fingers with his. "I'm not as ethical as you are."

The hell she wasn't. "I cannot believe you've ever before taken opposing counsel—"

Her free hand covered his mouth.

"I want to misstep *with you* a lot, Dunstan. This is a problem. We're in a small jurisdiction, and the family law bar is smaller yet. We should have opposed each other at least twice a year, and why that hasn't happened, I do not know."

"You were willing to toss aside your license to practice law to have at my earlobes, and now you're not willing to pass on the occasional case because I might oppose you? You'll let yourself have a taste of something wonderful, then go back to chicken salad on wilted lettuce?"

"I had another option in mind."

Options were good. The more options, the greater the likelihood of settlements. "I'm listening." And holding her hand too tightly.

"I was hoping Louise would change her mind about art school, but she's off to New York next semester, or somewhere. My office is set up for two attorneys, and I hate to do the billing."

He brought her hand to his lips and kissed her knuckles. "You are a fraud, Jane DeLuca. A lovely, brilliant little fraud. Beneath that calculating legal mind beats the heart of a true romantic."

"I really do hate the billing."

A true, honest romantic. He tucked her hair back, the better to see the woman he loved. "Are you sure about this? Because clearly, my house has room for a home office."

She regarded their joined hands solemnly. "Do you have a utility closet?"

"Aye. How do you feel about scheduled sex?"

She glanced at the clock. "I'm okay with it, occasionally. Maybe around 2:53 p.m.?"

"I had 2:55 p.m. in mind because we have one more item to cover in our first partners' meeting. Will you come to Scotland with me over the holidays? Meet the family, dandle a few bairnies, flirt with Uncle Donald?"

"Yes." She inched her chair closer. "This all feels very sudden, and very right."

He gave up her hand for the pleasure of putting his arms around her. "That it does, but you should be warned, I'm no' asking you to travel home with me simply to show off Scotland."

"I'd love to see Scotland."

"I'm scheduling a proposal, too, Jane DeLuca. I want to propose to you on my home turf, when I can tell my family if you've accepted and have my choice of fine whiskeys to console me if you turn me down."

She kissed his cheek. "Does the conference room door lock?"

"Aye. Why?"

"Because it's 2:55 p.m., and I've had ideas about this conference table since I first laid eyes on it."

Dunstan locked the door, and they held the longest partners' meeting in the history of Damson County bar association.

ABOUT THE AUTHOR

New York Times and *USA Today* bestselling author Grace Burrowes hit the bestseller lists with her debut, *The Heir*, followed by *The Soldier*, *Lady Maggie's Secret Scandal*, and *Lady Eve's Indiscretion*. *The Heir* was a *Publishers Weekly* Best Book of 2010, *The Soldier* was a *Publishers Weekly* Best Spring Romance of 2011, *Lady Sophie's Christmas Wish* won Best Historical Romance of the Year from RT Reviewers' Choice Awards, *Lady Louisa's Christmas Knight* was a *Library Journal* Best Book of 2012, and *The Bridegroom Wore Plaid*, the first in her trilogy of Scotland-set Victorian romances, was a *Publishers Weekly* Best Book of 2012. All of her historical romances have received extensive praise, including several starred reviews from *Publishers Weekly* and *Booklist*. *Darius*, the first in her groundbreaking Regency series The Lonely Lords, was named one of iBookstore's Best Romances of 2013.

Grace is a practicing family law attorney and lives in rural Maryland. She loves to hear from her readers and can be reached through her website at graceburrowes.com.

Ready for more happily ever after from Grace Burrowes? Please consider the first novel in The Sweetest Kisses contemporary romance series:

A Single Kiss (January 2015)
New attorney Hannah Stark has set her sights on corporate law to assure her a career of paperwork, predictability, and conservative suits. Contracts, finance, and the art of the deal sing to her, while the mess and misery of the courtroom do not. But her daughter needs to eat, so when Hannah is offered a temporary position in a small town firm's domestic relations department, she reluctantly accepts.

Trent Knightley is mightily drawn to his newest associate, though Hannah is as protective of her privacy as she is competent. When their friendship and attraction heat up, secrets Hannah is desperate to keep will put her heart and Trent's hopes in double jeopardy.

Grace also enthusiastically recommends:

The Rogue Spy (November 4, 2014) by Joanna Bourne, fifth novel the award-winning Spymaster Series.

For years he'd lived a lie. It was time to tell the truth . . . even if it cost him the woman he loved. Ten years ago he was a boy, given the name Thomas Paxton and sent by Revolutionary France to infiltrate the British Intelligence Service. Now his sense of honor brings him back to London, alone and unarmed, to confess. But instead of facing the gallows, he's given one last impossible assignment to prove his loyalty. Lovely, lying, former French spy Camille Leyland is dragged from her safe rural obscurity by threats and blackmail. Dusting off her spy skills, she sets out to track down a ruthless French fanatic and rescue the innocent victim he's holding—only to find an old colleague already on the case. Pax.Old friendship turns to new love, and as Pax and Camille's dark secrets loom up from the past, Pax is left with a choice—go rogue from the Service or lose Camille forever...

Or treat yourself to Grace's favorite Scottish contemporary romance, **To Scotland With Love**, first novel in Patience Griffin's Kilts and Quilts series.

Visit Grace's website at www.GraceBurrowes.com for more titles, excerpts, and updates, or for all the latest news, sign up for Grace's newsletter at GraceBurrowes.com/contact.php.

54453001R00059

Made in the USA
Columbia, SC
31 March 2019